# THE NURSE AND THE NEONATAL SURGEON

Sacred Heart Children's Hospital: Book 1

Liza Collins

Copyright © 2024 Liza Collins

All rights reserved

The characters and events portrayed in this book are fictitious. Any similarity to real persons, living or dead, is coincidental and not intended by the author.

No part of this book may be reproduced, or stored in a retrieval system, or transmitted in any form or by any means, electronic, mechanical, photocopying, recording, or otherwise, without express written permission of the publisher.

ISBN: 9798338238790

# CONTENTS

Title Page
Copyright
| | |
|---|---:|
| CHAPTER ONE | 1 |
| CHAPTER TWO | 13 |
| CHAPTER THREE | 25 |
| CHAPTER FOUR | 47 |
| CHAPTER FIVE | 58 |
| CHAPTER SIX | 69 |
| CHAPTER SEVEN | 77 |
| CHAPTER EIGHT | 91 |
| CHAPTER NINE | 103 |
| CHAPTER TEN | 119 |
| CHAPTER ELEVEN | 134 |
| CHAPTER TWELVE | 143 |
| CHAPTER THIRTEEN | 156 |
| CHAPTER FOURTEEN | 175 |
| CHAPTER FIFTEEN | 186 |

| | |
|---|---|
| CHAPTER SIXTEEN | 197 |
| CHAPTER SEVENTEEN | 205 |
| CHAPTER EIGHTEEN | 217 |
| CHAPTER NINETEEN | 230 |
| EPILOGUE | 238 |
| About The Author | 243 |
| Sacred Heart Children's Hospital | 245 |
| Books By This Author | 247 |

Sacred Heart Children's Hospital
Hampstead
London Borough of Camden

Little Neptune Neonatal Unit

# CHAPTER ONE

♥

*Nina*

I was a mere two hours into my night shift when the alarm blared from nursery room one; the high-dependency room where we looked after the very sickest of babies. Instantly, I just knew it was one of mine.

Only twenty-six-weeks gestation and small enough to fit in the palm of my hand, Sofia was fragile to say the least. When I'd left her after a very small milk feed via her nasogastric tube, she was calm and settled, with pink skin and excellent sats. She had been progressing wonderfully, and we hoped she'd be going home on schedule within just a few months.

But the alarm blaring now meant something was very, very wrong. It meant my baby was collapsing. If we didn't stabilise her quickly, we could lose her.

"Doctor Hartcliffe!" I bellowed as I turned and fled to nursery room one. I needn't have done so; he was already on the way, bursting from nursery room three where he'd been doing his rounds after surgery. Dr Bellamy and Dr Hurst came running too; knowing the ward like the backs of their hands, they were surrounding the baby's cot within moments.

"Oxygen dropping rapidly," said Doctor Hartcliffe. "Start resuscitation."

I didn't need to hear my own name to know it was me he was addressing. The neonatal ward was a well-oiled machine, and we all knew our places. Mine was with Sofia, who had turned an awful shade of grey and was worsening by the second. Dr Hartcliffe monitored her with a stethoscope to the chest while I administered the puffs of air, holding the mask firmly over Sofia's tiny mouth and nose while the machine helped her to breathe.

Dr Hartcliffe prodded and massaged her belly with two fingers; she was so tiny that the width of his fingers almost spanned her entire abdomen. Very gradually, her oxygen saturations began to correct with the assistance of the machine.

"When was her last feed?" asked Dr Hartcliffe.

"9.32 p.m., 20mls of breast milk administered."

"Did she feed well?"

"Like a champion," I said, "I had no concerns whatsoever."

"Fuck," said Dr Hartcliffe under his breath. "It could be an issue with the hernia repair. Could be maladjustment to the medication."

Mercifully, Sofia's skin colour was returning

from the deathly grey pallor it had taken on, but she wasn't out of the woods yet.

"Allergies?" asked Doctor Bellamy.

"She's a twenty-six-weeker. That's anyone's guess," said Dr Hartcliffe, his handsome face looking flushed, his brow tightly knitted in concern. "If we can stabilise her long enough, we'll get her under a scan and see what's what."

Doctor Hurst took bloods and urine and ran from the room to get them off to toxicology. As I looked down at Sofia's tiny, cherubic face, a feeling came over me that something else wasn't right. She appeared to be frowning. I pulled the mask away in time for her to gag and release a sudden gush of white fluid.

"Projectile vomit, approximately 20mls," I said, wiping the excess from Sofia's mouth. Her eyes screwed up as she let out a long, frustrated gargle, turning a shade of crimson. She balled her tiny fists and wriggled her sparrow-legs as she made her discomfort known to us.

"Good, good," said Dr Hartcliffe, moving his stethoscope around her abdomen. "Any mucus?"

"Small amount, 5ml," I said, hazarding a guess before I could measure it.

"Oxygen saturations are looking good. No fever, no indication of infection barring the vomit," said Dr Bellamy, holding one hand on the monitor as he peered intently at its blinking screen.

"I'm telling you all now" said Dr Hartcliffe. "If

it's that new-grade mesh that's the culprit, heads will roll."

Sofia had been operated on directly after birth to repair a stomach hernia; it should have been straight-forward, an operation they'd performed hundreds of times – and as far as the team knew, it had been.

"It happens," said Dr Bellamy. "Neonates at this level of gestation are prone –"

"You think I don't know that?" Dr Hartcliffe barked, looking up at Dr Bellamy as if he could tear his head off with his bare hands. "You think I need educating? By you?"

"No, of course not," said Dr Bellamy, flushing from the neck up.

I couldn't help but feel sorry for Tom, who was only eager to show-off his knowledge for brownie points. He was a junior to Dr Hartcliffe – Mr Hartcliffe, really, given he was a senior neonatal surgeon – and boy, did Dr Hartcliffe let him know it. Dr Bellamy was barely 30 and considered a fresh face amongst the neonatal doctors, especially at Sacred Heart Children's Hospital, where surgeons were flown in from all over the world to treat specialist cases. He was small fry, practically still a student.

Dr Hartcliffe was in his mid-to-late-forties and renowned for his skills world-wide. He had one hell of an ego, and a vicious temper, with no fear whatsoever of showing it.

"I only meant that you shouldn't blame your – " Dr Bellamy's voice trailed off with one flash of Dr Hartcliffe's heartless, piercing eyes. ' – s-self."

The penny finally dropped that he was better off monitoring the sats and keeping his mouth shut.

"When I want your opinion, I'll bloody-well ask for it," said Dr Hartcliffe, returning to his study of Sofia's abdomen. He breathed heavily through his nostrils for a moment like a bull. "No looping, intestines soft," he muttered. "Fluids?"

"30ml, " said Dr Bellamy. "Blood pressure stable."

"Good. Good," said Dr Hartcliffe, removing the stethoscope. "If it's the mesh, those bastards won't hear the last of it from me when I find out what's gone wrong this time."

Sofia was stable, for now, but she would require constant monitoring until Dr Hartcliffe could get her scanned. The atmosphere was heavy, intense, with all present knowing that there was a possibility that poor Sofia would need to be put back under anaesthetic so any issues with her mesh could be repaired. That came with its own set of risks.

"Have the parents been contacted?"

"They're on-site in one of the parent suites," I said, breathlessly. "I'll run for them now. It's quicker than ringing down."

"Tell them we're scanning her now, and if she needs surgery they'll get a minute to see her before we take her down," said Dr Hartcliffe. "Get running."

I didn't need telling twice. Dr Hartcliffe took over with the resuscitation machine while I turned on my heels and ran, flying down the corridor to the stairwell, where I took the steps two at a time.

Parents were invited to visit the ward at all hours, day or night, even for the high-dependency babies. Sofia's mother had delivered her milk at the beginning of my shift and witnessed her feeding, knowing that closeness and skin-to-skin contact was important as much as possible for babies – especially premies like Sofia. Both her mother and father had held her tiny hand, too, watching over her as she settled for the night.

I'd sent them away to get some much-needed rest, and now I would have to wake them and usher them to the pre-op room in their pyjamas. My chest felt tight as I realised I was about to instil absolute fear into their hearts when I delivered the news. Nausea, anxiety, desperation would take over them as they waited, and it wouldn't abate until Sofia was in recovery and fully stabilised.

It was a part of my job that was always difficult, but the news would be much better coming from me than ice-cold Dr Hartcliffe. He was a gorgeous silver-fox, tall, with a built frame and icy blue-green eyes that melted many a student nurse's heart, especially combined with his dark hair flecked with grey. His personality was something else entirely; he was cold, proficient, and deadly to anybody that crossed him.

There was a reason he was world-renowned for his skill; he never made mistakes and yielded impeccable results for his newborn patients. That is, until things changed, and new technologies were introduced – ones that *he* didn't have experience in, and didn't yet fully understand. Dr Hartcliffe didn't trust a damn one of them, and had recently found himself faced with the possibility that he might just make a mistake – the new mesh for hernia repair in neonates being one of them.

As I hurried through the parents' suite and found their bedroom, my heart was pounding. I composed myself, determined not to betray a single emotion and give them any idea that Sofia's life was in danger. They would be given the facts, but I would not influence them; they'd struggle enough on their own without me adding to their fears. It would be my job to calm them and reassure them that Sofia was in the very best hands.

I knew Dr Hartcliffe could keep his composure long enough to do the necessary repairs, even if it did turn out to be the fault of the dreaded mesh. It was the aftermath that terrified me, when he no longer held a tiny life in his hands, and could let loose on the staff with his snarling, tiger-like fury.

♥

It had been a long, dreadful night of waiting

on news of Sofia while I tended the neonates in rooms two and three. When she was wheeled back to nursery room one, I was elated to learn in the de-brief that the scan had merely showed a swelling that had put pressure on her digestive passage, causing difficulties with her airways as well as producing the projectile vomit. The mesh was secure and intact, and there had been no need at all for any surgical intervention. A course of antibiotics, fluids, and careful monitoring should ensure that Sofia didn't experience a sudden collapse like that again.

By the time I was clocking off at 8.00 a.m., I felt battered and bruised, weary from the rollercoaster of emotions myself and the staff had gone through. As I washed up in the locker room, I realised my neatly-fashioned bun was now a straggled mess of loose strands, and my cat-eyeliner had smudged in the corners of my eyes – no doubt from sweating. I was looking forward to getting back to my flat and having a hot shower before collapsing into bed. I might even have time, I realised, to stuff down a victory cup of tea and a slice of toast. My stomach growled for dinner, even though it was breakfast time; such was my ruined night-shift-worker's body clock.

The last person I wanted to bump into as I entered the hallway feeling grimy and wrecked was Dr Hartcliffe. In my eagerness to leave after what was a hefty handover, I made a brisk right-turn out of the changing room and slammed directly into the brick wall that was our leading neonatal surgeon. He scowled, his eyes cutting a line right through me.

"I'm so sorry, Doctor," I said, taking a couple of steps back. When he didn't move, I cleared my throat. "*Pardon me*."

"What's your first name again?" he asked. He had a harsh, no-nonsense Yorkshire accent and a rugged overnight stubble on his face. It would be irresistible if he wasn't such an arsehole.

"Nina," I said, sighing. "I'm sorry, I'm going to be late for my bus – "

"Don't you give me the brush-off, Ms Dorrington. I'm talking to you."

I cocked an eyebrow and looked up at the impressive man who was bullying me in the hallway, his massive frame blocking my only way out. I was tempted to remind him he wasn't technically my boss, but I knew that'd only invite more attitude – and he was capable of more attitude than a toddler who'd dropped their ice cream.

"Was there anything in particular you needed to talk to me about?"

"Yeah," he said, folding his arms. His shirt buttons were strained against his swelling chest, as if they might blow right off. Dr Hartcliffe had the overall appearance of a bear made to wear a shirt and trousers, with all too much muscle and fur stuffed into awkward places – or like a seasoned rugby player trussed up in a wedding suit.

"I wanted to tell you that you did a smashing job, back there."

I blinked rapidly. "What?"

"When you moved the mask. You anticipated that vomit, didn't you?"

I paused, thinking on it. "I studied her face. I could tell something was about to happen."

"You saved her from choking," he said. "You did well there. I'm impressed with your observation."

I straightened myself from my slouching position and managed a smile. I wasn't usually one for compliments; I was a nurse, and I was doing my job. It didn't require any compliments. But coming from him – well, that stumped me on all levels.

"T-t-thank you, Dr Hartcliffe," I said.

"Try not to sound too astonished," he said. "I'm not always a complete bastard, you know. Them lot would have you think I was," he said, gesturing with a nod of his head to some invisible party. "I've had HR breathing down my neck for years about my conduct with the nursing staff."

I could easily believe it, but I wasn't going to dare say it. I chewed my lip, wondering how on earth I would get around his bulk. My stomach was grumbling fiercely, and I had a long way to get home.

"If it's all right with you – "

"If you think you're going home, you can think again. There's a breakfast in the canteen with your name on it. Don't tell me you're not starving after a night like that? I know I am."

My instinct was to instantly shut him down – no way was I going to spend a gruelling time across the table from him in the canteen, enduring his brash manners when really I wanted to be at home in my bed. But, my growling stomach had other plans, and it betrayed me. It gurgled and grumbled loud enough for Max to hear.

"I've actually got a banana in my bag," I began, feeling foolish and blushing furiously.

"Bore off," he said, clapping me on the shoulder. He jogged me so hard I nearly lost my balance. "There's nowt on you and you're clearly starving. My treat, how's that? I can thank a member of staff for their exemplary observations, can't I?"

"Well..."

"That is, unless I'm making you uncomfortable?" he said, pulling his hand away very suddenly. I thought I noted a sadness in his blue-green eyes, as if realising for the hundredth time that he had invaded another human being's personal space. "If you don't fancy it, feel free to say so."

I snorted with laughter, wondering if he had any self-awareness inside him at all. His concerned face changed to one of amusement as I laughed, and his large shoulders relaxed.

"You're not making me uncomfortable," I said. "But I really do need to get home. Come on – I'll let you buy me a cup of tea and a bit of toast for me to take out with me. How's that?"

"If you say so," he said gruffly, unfolding his arms. I had the feeling he wasn't used to anybody holding firm or standing their ground with him, even over something as daft as breakfast.

# CHAPTER TWO
♥

*Max*

She was a stubborn little witch, I'd give her that. Offer a tired nurse a free breakfast and that was the thanks I could expect. Still, I could tell by the way her sleepy chocolate-brown eyes lit up when I'd complimented her that she really did appreciate the sentiment, even if she found me a bit overbearing. She wouldn't be the first; most people, especially women in our industry, found me to be brash, overconfident, and domineering.

Some, you might say, liked that quality in me – especially if a quick fling was involved. Others, like this young nurse – not so much. No matter. I meant what I said, and a breakfast after a difficult night was my way of showing my appreciation – she could like it or bloody-well lump it.

I led the way to the lifts going up to the canteen, and Nina was eerily silent as she stood beside me. She was a small curvy thing, late-twenties, without a scrap of make-up except for some eye-liner that looked like a kid had applied it – but she'd had a hard shift, just as I had, and I certainly wasn't looking or smelling my best. I shuffled uneasily in my shirt – I so hated wearing these bastard uncomfortable outfits – knowing I could use a wash and a spray of deodorant myself. I cleared my throat and noticed how she flinched at the sound of me, as if a gun had just gone off. It was unusual for a neonatal nurse to be so nervous, but then, of course, she was probably only nervous because she was around me.

Sadly, I had that effect on people – even my colleagues, who should bloody-well know better. We're a team; always, the team comes first, or else we'll crumble. It would hurt me to think that any one of them were really afraid of me.

"Are you cold?" I asked. It was still winter, after all. Spring was a way off yet. I noticed how she hugged herself as if to keep her arms from getting chilly, even though she was wearing her tunic and a cardigan over the top of that.

"No, I'm fine," she said, smiling. Her eyes were dark and sparkling, with long eyelashes and tired bags beneath her eyes. Somehow her tiredness made her look beautiful; over-worked, weary, ready for bed.

Perhaps it was the bed part that caught my attention. Yeah, it had to be – I kicked myself for being so dreadfully sex-obsessed. With her hair a tousled mess, she looked as if she'd not long got out from between the sheets, or desperately needed to get in them – and I couldn't help wondering if I could help her there.

*No, you pig, leave it out – she's far too young for you,* my inner voice told me in an admonishing tone. *What do you have - 15 years on her, at least? She could do better than an old dog like you.*

We got out at the canteen and I ordered myself a full English with tea, squash, the works. Nina eyed the offerings uneasily, as if overwhelmed by the choices.

"Just toast and butter for me," she said. "Oh, and a cup of tea would be lovely."

"We can share a pot," I said, which for some bizarre reason made her blush. "What? I fancy a brew myself – it's wasteful not to buy a pot for two."

"I'm really very late for my bus," she said, and I detected her irritation.

"All right, all right. I'll get yours in a takeaway cup."

Why was she so determined not to speak to me like a human being? I could understand that she wanted to leave, but if she was really so against it, why didn't she just tell me straight to my face to bugger off?

We took a seat close to the door, which annoyed me because I liked being by the window where I could watch the people far below. But I was sensing that she wasn't just being shy, or that she didn't really have to leave in such a hurry – it was me. I was bothering her, and she wanted an easy route out.

"You're not afraid of me, are you, Nina?"

She removed the lid from her cardboard cup of tea and blew gently on the surface, letting the steam rise up.

"No," she said. "Of course not."

She didn't meet my eyes. I didn't believe her.

"Look at me, pet," I said, in as soft a voice as I could stand to use. I was a loud, brash lad – always had been – and I didn't know how else to be. I only knew that some people found me *too much*, and I didn't know how to be less. Nina looked up at me, and immediately her cheeks flushed pink again. But her eyes met mine, firmly, as if in challenge.

*Bloody 'eck*, I thought – it couldn't be that she actually *likes me*, could it? Then why was she fighting me at every step, and making every effort to avoid me?

"No, I'm not afraid of you," she repeated. "But I am really very tired and I've got a long journey home. I'm so used to just rushing out of this place that it feels wrong to be delaying it."

"You're on your four days off, aren't you?"

"Yes," she said. "But it's my routine. I get home as quickly as possible because the buses can be so unreliable."

There came a loud pattering sound. I glanced up from the breakfast I was already inhaling and saw that the sky outside was a bleak, chalky grey, and thick globules of rain were hammering against the window. That would be a grim wait at the bus stop.

"Well do me a favour and relax a little bit. You're here now – I could cut the bloody tension with a knife. It's ruining my meal." I winked gently, trying to show her that I wasn't being serious. Her shoulders did visibly relax, then, and her hands cupped her tea as if she was okay to stay a while – not so keen as she had been to dart out the door the moment it was socially acceptable to do so.

"I'm sorry," she said. "I'm just so used to doing everything a certain way. I hardly ever socialise with anybody on the ward anymore."

"Nowt to be sorry about," I said, gulping down my tea and pushing my plate away. One of the canteen staff collected it on her trolley; I gave her a grateful smile. She'd worked here so long that she felt like my mother sometimes, always cleaning up after me and bringing me another mug of tea. "But I did notice. That's why I asked you here – I realised we've barely said two words to one another in – how many years has it been?"

"Just three," said Nina. "And I did have my student placement here, too. It's just so hard – we're always so busy."

"You didn't pick an easy nursing career, that goes without saying," I said. My chest didn't feel so tight now, and I was breathing easier once I could see she was relaxed. I hadn't realised how affected

I'd been by her apparent reluctance to spend any time with me, but it was like a weight had lifted.

"I just loved working with the little ones," she said. "And supporting the parents. I get so much from it. After I did my placement here, I knew I just had to work with babies – especially the premies."

"Aye," I said. "If you'd asked me when I was a student whether I'd work with babies, I'd have laughed in your face."

Her eyes widened in shock. "Really?"

"Really," I said. "I wasn't planning on sticking around here for love nor money. I had it all set in my mind – I was going to move to Los Angeles and specialise in plastic surgery. I was going to make my millions and give all the celebs in Hollywood new faces."

"Then what happened? Why did you stay?" Now she sounded really invested, with passion in her voice. Now *that's* what I wanted to hear.

"My ex-wife," I said, with a grim tone of voice. "I had to choose between her or my Hollywood dreams, and she won. She wanted to stay in the UK, raise a big family, become a GP. I thought love was more important – bloody idiot I was – and I chose to stay, get married, become a family man. It wasn't meant to be. She couldn't have kids, which wasn't a problem for me, but over time we drifted apart. One day she said she didn't feel the spark anymore, and we called it quits."

I felt uncomfortable when I realised how I'd

rambled on, over-sharing as-per-bloody-usual, but Nina looked transfixed, actually interested in my story.

"Just like that?"

I shrugged, feeling the old familiar soreness in my heart – it hurt for just a moment, and then subsided. "I think she had her heart set on kids, and adoption would be our only route. I was against it at the time. I had my career to focus on, and she had hers, and I just couldn't see how we'd have the time to focus on that process. Eventually we got stuck in our own routines – her at the community practice, me at the hospital, and we became housemates. It happens."

Nina was frowning, like she was thinking deeply about something I'd said.

"What is it?" I asked.

"You didn't want kids?" she asked, looking perplexed.

"If I'm honest, no. Can't stand the little sods, always getting under your feet, wrecking your house, screaming...no, it wasn't for me. But I would have done it for her because I was in love. Unfortunately it wasn't meant to be, and I wanted to move on. She couldn't. She blamed herself, resentment grew...look, take my advice – don't get bloody married. Save yourself the torment and focus on yourself."

I was getting flustered now, feeling mixed up from talking about the past in such detail. I'd planned to get to know her better, and here I was once again yapping about my chuffin' self. Nina didn't bat an eyelid; she looked intrigued, genuinely interested. It was flattering.

"But you're a neonatal surgeon. I just assumed you must love kids," said Nina.

I smiled, finding her naivety endearing. "It's an entirely different kettle of fish all together. My job is to fix them, get them well, and send them off to grow up and live their lives – the big plus being that I get to do my job and give them back at the end of it."

Nina laughed, taking a long sip of her tea. Well, at least she appeared to be enjoying my company.

"You surprise me," she said. I took it from her warm smile that I was surprising her in a positive way.

"Anyway, enough about me," I said. "There is another reason I've dragged you in here today. Some little birdies told me you'll be leaving soon to go to Uganda, of all places?"

Nina blushed, casting her eyes down. "I am. I'm so sorry. It's not that I'm not dedicated to my work here, I really am – but they're so desperate for nurses over there and I –"

I held my hands up as if in surrender, stopping her mid-sentence. "You've got nothing to apologise for!"

"I know, I know. I just – I feel like I'm abandoning Sacred Heart, that's all. I feel guilty about leaving," she said, making a deep sigh.

"I think it's dead brave, what you're doing. I wish you all the best with it. We'll miss your talent here, of course – and you'll be welcomed back whenever your placement finishes. How long are you out there for?"

She looked relieved, but she had tears in her eyes. I could tell she really would miss being here.

"Just a year to start with, and then possibly an extension to two. The Trust granted me a secondment, so I'll be able to come back again. It's just the thought of leaving everything behind has suddenly given me cold feet," she said.

"Follow your dreams, Nina, wherever they take you. Don't get stuck like me. I should be kicking back in my swimming pool in Beverley Hills," I said, sounding more angry than I intended to.

"But instead you're here, saving the innocent little lives of babies," she said, rolling her eyes. Wait, was she mocking me? "Poor you! What a horrible life choice you've made!"

I felt my face go scarlet – the cheeky cow. "Hang on just a minute, lass – "

"It must be so difficult being swooned at and appearing in all the world's media for being a hero, Dr Hartcliffe," she said, but she was smiling, indicating at least that she was joking. Hey, she'd become very comfortable all of a sudden – comfortable enough to mock me. I simmered down, realising we were making progress, even if it *was* at my expense.

"First of all, you cheeky mare, my name's Max. You can call me that. And second of all...I know just how lucky I am, to be doing what I'm doing. I don't regret it for even a second. I was a working class boy – my dad worked in construction and my mum was a part-time receptionist. I was fortunate enough to pass my exams and get into the grammar school, and two years into that, I was awarded a scholarship to attend a boarding school in Herfordshire.

"I got a top-class education when my parents had barely two pennies to rub together. Believe me, when I made it to medical school, I knew how arsehole-lucky I was, and I still do. Boys like me didn't become doctors, not where I was from." I took a deep breath, realising I'd done it once again – over-shared, told the poor cow my life story when she hadn't asked for it.

But again, I was surprised to see her looking at me with real interest, as if she could listen to more. Surely, I was imagining that?

"I'm sorry if I seemed like I was being rude," she said. "Of course you deserve every bit of praise you get."

"And so do you, miss international-nurse. I'd heard good things about you, and today I saw just how on-the-ball you are. We'll miss you when you bugger off to Uganda," I said. "And another thing, Nina –"

"What is it?"

"Stop fucking apologising," I said. "Weak people apologise all the time. You're not weak, and you've nowt to apologise for, so stop doing it."

She nodded, finally taking a bite of her toast. She agreed from behind a mouthful of hot buttered bread. "Got it," she said, swallowing.

"Listen, Nina - it's pouring outside. Will you let me offer you a lift home?" I asked, jerking my head towards the window panes that were streaming water. The weather had really turned nasty, and I didn't feel right making her wait at a bus stop when it was me who'd held her up in the first place.

"Oh, no, please – that really won't be necessary," she began, shaking her head. I was annoyed already, knowing she was going to give me grief over something as small as the offer of a lift home.

"Nina, accept the bloody offer, will you? It's pouring, you'll catch your death!"

"Really, please, it wouldn't be right – "

"It's a lift, not a poxy proposal," I said, feeling something vibrate in my pocket. Nina's vibrated too, and then in unison they both let off their bleeping sound. Our pagers were firing off because a crash call had gone out, and we were still on-site. It meant we were obligated to spring into action, and already my heart started thumping, my adrenaline kicking off like a greyhound bolting after a rabbit.

Our eyes met as we both jumped up from

our seats and ran for the corridor, knowing that neither one of us would need to explain anything – we would just get up and run for it, hoping we made it in time.

# CHAPTER THREE
♥

*Nina*

It was Sofia again.

As we burst into the ward, we were met with a throng of doctors and nurses from the morning shift, fighting to keep Sofia alive. I immediately began assisting the nursing team while Dr Hartcliffe shoved his way in, insisting on taking over her resuscitation. She was his baby, as far as he was concerned, and he was going to see her through.

Babies so very rarely collapsed like this at Sacred Heart. Although they were fragile and prone to all kinds of complications and infections, it was out of the ordinary for a baby to be fighting so hard against treatment. Sofia's little body was in the wars, and we had to hope our efforts could overpower whatever it was that was trying to harm her.

It was a long, gruelling day. No sooner had Sofia stabilised and I'd brought her parents back in, than she was whisked away again to theatre. A scan and bloods had indicated possible sepsis. Despite her course of medication, the swelling had only gotten worse, and her poor body was drowning. The infected tissue had turned into an abscess, and the team had no choice but to remove it.

It meant more trauma on Sofia's tiny body, and a rising potential that she would lose her life. I comforted the parents while the surgery was undertaken, fighting through my own exhaustion to ensure that they were never left alone or without communication about Sofia's progress.

When Doctor Hartcliffe returned to the quiet room where I was waiting with Sofia's parents, he looked shattered, destroyed, his eyes bloodshot from exhaustion – but I could tell instantly that the surgery had been a success.

"We located the source of the infection and we've successfully removed it," he said. "It'll be touch and go, and the next twenty-four hours will be crucial, but she's stable and will be ready to be moved back to HDU soon," he said. Sofia's parents cried out in joy and hugged one another, tears streaming down their faces. Sofia's mum hugged me, and her dad shook Dr Hartcliffe's hand.

I noticed Dr Hartcliffe accepted the gesture, but looked distant, shaken, as if he felt he didn't deserve it – not at least until Sofia was officially safe, and that could take days.

"You saved our baby's life," said Sofia's father, his voice breaking as he squeezed Doctor Hartcliffe's hand in his.

"I'm just glad we got to the site of the infection in time," said Dr Hartcliffe, pressing his mouth together in a firm line that wasn't quite a smile. I understood him – he would smile when Sofia was sent home to be with her family, and not before.

When they wheeled Sofia in, I made it my personal responsibility to settle her into nursery room one and give her the first milk feed. Then I would hand back to the day shift nursing team and leave her in their care. It was getting so late; nearly 7.00 p.m., almost 12 hours since I should have gone home. The day shift would be handing over to the night shift within another hour. My body shook with exhaustion, and I could feel a cold sweat on the small of my back. I longed to get home, throw myself into a quick shower and then collapse into bed. But there would be a long, gruelling bus ride first, and it was storming outside. The wind howled like something from a horror movie, whistling through the leaves and swaying the treetops. It wasn't going to be pleasant.

I decided I would treat myself to a very expensive but very necessary cab. I was grateful, in that moment, as I watched Sofia's parents look over her crib with an arm around one another's waist, that Dr Hartcliffe had done me a huge favour by inviting me to breakfast. Even that slice of toast and cup of tea had given me the energy to keep going, picking me up whenever duty wasn't enough to keep my eyes open and head alert.

Having already said my goodbyes, I planned to gently slip out of the room and let the oncoming staff take over. There came the gruff noise of a man clearing his throat in the hall. I wandered out, coming face-to-face with the man himself.

"Dr Hartcliffe!"

He rolled his blood-shot eyes. "Max. Call me Max, will you?"

"All right," I said, stifling a yawn. "Max it is. I'm afraid I couldn't possibly stay awake long enough to eat another meal in the canteen, and I bet you couldn't either."

"I'm not offering food – I'm here to offer you that lift."

I shuffled uneasily on my feet, listening to the howling of the wind outside. All right, the weather was ghastly – but it still felt wrong to accept a lift.

"I won't hear no for an answer," he said. "I'm not letting you wait at a bus stop in this weather. Besides, they've probably cancelled the service – there'll be a tree fallen somewhere, mark my words."

"Max, I really appreciate it, but I can take myself home. I'm a big girl," I said. "Besides, I live a good hour away by bus – won't you be going well out of your way?"

Max rolled his eyes. "Look, I'm getting in my warm comfy car within the next three minutes.

Have a look out that window in the hall and let me know if you'll be joining me. I'll be waiting down in the car park if you come to your senses," he said, tutting as he left.

I wandered sleepily to the hall and looked out at the city-scape cloaked in darkness, the rain hammering against the window panes. In the distance, sparks flew from an overhead cable being knocked about in the harsh winds.

He was right. I really did need to come to my senses – there was no way in hell I was going to stand around waiting for a bus or a cab when I could just hop into a waiting car. Besides, my body was close to collapsing – I needed rest, and this was the fastest way to get it.

Max, true to his word, was waiting for me in the dimly-lit car park. He drove a posh black Mercedes that smelled factory-fresh when I hopped into the passenger seat.

"Stick your postcode into the nav, will you?" he asked, selecting music on the touch-screen. "You all right with a bit of classic rock? I can't guarantee I won't fall asleep at the wheel unless I have it on." He winked, but I didn't want to risk the joke becoming a reality.

Besides, I loved classic rock.

The journey was arduous as the storm continued, and I stole fearful glances at Max as he wove his way through the increasing onslaught of wind and rain. Thankfully we'd made the best part of the journey while it was still bearable. Soon, it wouldn't be safe to continue. Even Max looked to be on high alert, glancing quickly between mirrors as his windscreen wipers struggled to keep up with the spray.

The storm wasn't the only reason I stole glances at Max. Up until this incredibly difficult shift, I'd only ever known him as terrifying, grouchy Dr Hartcliffe, a gruff oversized bloke who you absolutely didn't want to mess with. Now I saw a different side to him; like a tired grizzly bear, searching for a cave to curl up in. He'd saved Sofia's life and hopped in his car as if all he'd done was rearrange a filing cabinet or fire off some emails. He looked shattered, but he was capable, in control, unrattled. I admired him.

That, and he looked super hot when he was sleepy – especially with that gritty five o'clock shadow, and the lazy look it gave his oceanic eyes. His grey and black hair was a mess, and he had bags under his eyes, but his strong arms looked so warm and inviting that I could just imagine curling up inside them.

Maybe that last part was the exhaustion talking.

"Here we are," said Max, finally pulling up outside my flat.

As the wind picked up, another onslaught of rain attacked the car, trapping us inside a monsoon. I felt dreadful when I saw the annoyance on Max's face as he realised that he wouldn't be getting anywhere in this weather, and he certainly wouldn't be getting any shut-eye.

"I can't thank you enough for this, Max. Really, I can't." I found I had to raise my voice above the howling wind.

"Don't mention it," he said, peering unsuccessfully out of his windscreen.

Then I realised, all of a sudden, that I *could* thank him. It would feel highly inappropriate in any other circumstance, but given our dreadful double-shift, his exhaustion, and the danger of driving in weather like this, I actually felt it'd be unreasonable not to make the offer I was about to make.

"Crash at my place," I said, suddenly emboldened by duty.

"You what?" He chuckled, gruff and low. The sound gave me goosebumps.

"You can sleep in my flat. Come on, look at the weather – you're not going anywhere in this, and you're exhausted."

He paused, glancing at the passenger-seat window and windscreen , both views completely obscured by sheets of streaming water.

"I'd be in your way," he said, looking doubtful but completely shattered nonetheless.

"Please, Max. If you try and leave in this weather you'll have an accident and it'll be all my fault," I said.

"Rubbish," he said dismissively. "I've driven in worse than this."

I cocked an eyebrow, and he had the good grace to smirk. He absolutely hadn't driven in worse than this before, because that would be impossible.

"All right, maybe not quite this bad," he said. "But I can't impose on you– not when I insisted on driving you."

I pressed my lips together in a firm line, wondering how I could convince him that it wasn't an imposition, or creepy, or any of that – it was merely a matter of safety.

"All right – suppose you didn't get hurt, but somebody else did? Suppose they couldn't see you, crashed right into you and killed themselves, while you got off without a scratch? Then what?"

Max's eyes opened wide. "Yep, you've a fair point there."

"Then come on in before it gets worse out here," I said, struggling to force the car door open against the onslaught of rain.

Even as we dashed to my front door and I struggled with the key in the lock, Max towered over me and asked, "Are you absolutely sure?"

"Yes!" I hissed, finally getting the door open. I was grateful for my own fastidious cleaning schedule as we walked in, knowing that my humble home was at least fit to receive guests. Not that I ever had time for any with my schedule.

"Listen, the bathroom is through there," I said, pointing to my bedroom. "I'll set you up in the living room with blankets. It's not the comfiest sofa I'm afraid – it's a futon for when my mother visits, but the mechanism got jammed and now it's just an uncomfortable couch. You take a shower while I do that and I'll have one after while you get settled in here."

Max shifted uncomfortably on the spot, his enormous body taking up most of the hallway. I didn't feel any discomfort at all; I was in my domain now.

"And take your shoes off before you go any further," I said, leaving to fetch the blankets from the ottoman at the foot of my bed. It had been my granny's; it was old and threadbare but I cherished it.

"Yes, miss!" he said, slipping off his Chelsea boots. As I returned with blankets and two towels for him to take to the shower, he was neatly lining the boots up against the wall. Well, he was certainly trying to be considerate, even if he did make my flat look to be the size of a rabbit hole.

The humming sound of the running shower made comforting background noise, alongside that of the rain, as I made up the couch into a bed. It would be far, far too small for him, I realised, biting my lip. While I fretted about how to arrange the cushions to make it more comfortable, I heard the shower switch off and the door close. I decided

I would soften the blow with a cup of tea for him to take to his puny bed with him.

Just three minutes in the kitchen, and I was entering my bedroom with two steaming mugs of tea. That was *all* it took. Three minutes.

What greeted me was an enormous man sprawled on my side of the bed, snoring face-down into one of my pillows. He wore only his briefs and a clean white vest.

"Bollocks!" I hissed under my breath. I put the teas down on my chest of drawers by the window, realising I was now fated to sleep on the hideous, tiny, uncomfortably cramped couch.

Well, I thought – this was a fine way to thank me. But, in fairness, he had performed emergency surgery and pulled a double-shift. Although I'd worked damn hard myself, it would be hard to top emergency surgery. Sighing, I slouched my way to the shower and gasped at the mess he'd left behind. A towel was strewn, limp and sodden, across the lino. The mirror and window was steamed up, and he'd left his trousers and shirt hanging over my towel rail.

Now I remembered why I didn't usually allow men into my flat. There was at least enough hot water left for a shower, where I could scrub my body with soothing lavender soap and wash my hair twice through. As the water warmed my muscles, I felt them relaxing. I towelled my hair dry and combed it, dressing myself in fresh clean pyjamas. When I emerged, Max had turned onto his side, and was still snoring away.

It was dark, and suddenly I felt so exhausted I couldn't keep my eyelids from closing. *Blow the futon*, I thought. If he wanted to get precious about our proximity, then he could move to the living room. I was damn-well taking my bed. I gulped down a mouthful of lukewarm tea and threw myself down next to him, turning over so that my back was facing him. Instantly, I fell into a heavy, blissful sleep.

♥

As I gently drifted awake, I realised it was early. The room appeared blue-grey, cloaked in half-light as morning crept in. I could no longer hear the thudding of the rain hitting the window panes and car rooftops outside. A few birds chirped away in the trees.

Max was, thankfully, no longer snoring. I turned over and flinched as I came almost face-to-face with the sleeping bear that was our world-renowned neonatal surgeon. I stifled the urge to giggle at the inappropriateness; in seeing him here with his eyes shut, with their long lashes, his face relaxed in sleep. He was handsome in a rugged way, but here he looked almost sweet, like a baby.

I watched him, enjoying the opportunity to observe him without his knowledge. Soon I'd have to turf him out and make him drive back to his place, wherever that was, but for now, I was enjoying the view. He breathed so softly, his hard chest rising and falling with each gentle breath. He was laying on his side, with his arm folded beneath his head, his mouth squashed against the crook of his elbow. His lips looked plump and kissable, and I almost found myself longing to curl up against his body and feel for myself whether he had cast-iron pecs in there. As my eyes followed the line of his body, I settled my gaze on something that made my heart stop.

There inside his pants was one heck of an erection.

I could see its outline, its shape, its thickness against the taught fabric of his underwear. Max Hartcliffe had morning wood and he was in *my* bed. As I focused in, I could even see the waving line of a thick throbbing vein behind the thin material, indicating the extreme blood flow to his cock. I wondered what he was thinking about; whether it was just his normal morning erection, or if something – or someone – could have possibly been tantalising him in his dreams?

I flinched as his eyelids sprang open, feeling like I'd been caught with my hand in the cookie jar, even though I'd done nothing but look. Max's cool, clear eyes were drinking me in, without any hint of sleepiness. I realised, then, that he had been awake for some time.

"Morning," I said, sheepishly. I prayed I didn't have morning breath. I'd scrubbed my teeth and tongue hard the night before after my shower, but we'd been asleep for hours and hours. I could only hope I wasn't too unpleasant for him.

He certainly wasn't. He smelled faintly of soap and shampoo; a delicious and soothing scent that wafted over me as he shifted up, resting his head on a balled fist, with his elbow digging into his pillow.

"Morning yourself," he said.

He knew. He definitely knew I'd been staring at his dick. As the realisation hit me, Max began to laugh – just a low chuckle, but it confirmed my fears. I wasn't sure how best to hide my humiliation, so I abruptly turned over, making Max laugh even louder.

"I'm so sorry, pet – it's an occupational hazard when you share a bed with a man," he said. I felt him grab a pillow and heard him stuffing it between his legs. "I didn't mean for you to see that. I was just having a doze, and next thing I know, there you are with your eyes wide open…"

"It's okay," I said, rolling my face into my pillow as it burned roasting hot. "It's entirely my fault."

I turned over again to face him, only to be met with more laughter – softer now, though – as he spotted my pink skin. I breathed heavily, feeling faint – all kinds of emotions were swimming through me. Mostly I just wanted to move that pillow. Before I could hide my shame, I found my eyes fixating on the pillow as I imagined whipping it away.

"What're you..?" Max glanced down at the pillow, his brow knitting in confusion.

A boldness came over me as my groin ached and a longing stirred away inside my womb. I pulled my eyes up and met his gaze, asking questions with my eyes. Now Max looked embarrassed, running a hand through his messy dark hair.

"I won't be a moment in the bathroom, and then I'll...I'll be on my way, and...we can just forget...this incident." Max stuttered as he watched my hand reaching very gently for the pillow. I held the corner and looked up at him with hot cheeks, giving him the chance to say no. "I – you – you might not want to move that away just yet."

Curiosity took over me then. I pulled away the pillow and tossed it behind me, revealing an increased bulge, his erection bobbing outward at full mast.

"Oh Jesus," said Max, breathing heavily. "I'm so sorry, Nina. You were just so close to me, and I...god, just tell me to piss off and I will."

Now, I laughed. "I don't want you to," I said, practically salivating at the sight of such an enormous dick, just waiting for me. I'd broken up with my fiancé so long ago now that I'd almost forgotten what it was like to wake up beside a man who wanted me.

Despite my better judgement, all sense of caution and appropriateness just flew out of my mind. I found my hand drifting over the bed-sheet towards him, longing to give it just one stroke from behind the material of his briefs.

His breathing became ragged as he watched my hand.

"Nina," he said, almost groaning my name. "If you go any further, I won't be able to stop myself."

I met his eyes again, as if to seek permission, and he let his eyes close as he swallowed hard. Then I lifted my hand to his huge, hard column and felt it with my fingers, enjoying its size and girth. I slid my hand up the shaft and felt for its bulging head, so smooth and rounded in my palm. I squeezed and caressed it, moving down and up again. Max drew in a a long breath of air and released it slowly as I massaged him. I felt the blood swelling inside it as I teased. It bulged, bowing outward, from behind his restrictive briefs.

The cleft between my legs moistened and throbbed, and my nipples stiffened until they could cut glass. I watched Max's face become flushed in the cheeks as he – almost reluctantly – allowed himself to open his eyes and look at my breasts. Even inside my pyjamas, my nipples protruded obscenely.

I wasn't sure what on earth had come over me, but I was enjoying it; the sensual longing that I thought had been switched off inside me had suddenly returned. All I could think was...why waste this?

Max let his free hand drift to my top, his thumb and forefinger finding my left nipple and squeezing it. My belly flipped and I sucked in a sharp breath as pleasure shot between my nipple and my clitoris. Max rolled it between his fingers, toying with it, as he began to grind against my hand.

"Mm." I began to moan involuntarily, letting my long blonde hair fall about my face as I closed my eyes and enjoyed the sensation. I just couldn't believe it; here I was in bed with *Max Hartcliffe*. The oversized neonatal genius who ordinarily terrified me.

"Why don't you come close for a cuddle, love?" He said gently, drawing me into his arms.

I didn't need much more encouragement. I snuggled in close, letting his large biceps fold around me and his wide, warm hand cup my face as our lips met. He tasted delicious, warm, sensual; like a cinnamon roll made human. I wanted to eat him up. I found my tongue eagerly stroking his, and felt his hot breath as he sighed and let his hands roam my neck, my shoulders, sliding down to tweak my nipple once again.

I let my hand slip under his vest and felt the ripples of his abs, the hard mounds of his pecs, and his own stiff nipples. As my fingertips brushed them he groaned, pinching mine a little harder. His rock-hard erection was pressing now against my navel, and without thinking a moment longer, I let my hand slide lower to encourage his briefs down. I let his cock bounce free, feeling the clean smooth head against my tummy. We continued devouring one another's mouths, slowly, deliberately, as Max pulled down my trousers and knickers with them, and I shrugged off my pyjama top. We paused so Max could lift his vest over his head and toss it away, while I pulled his briefs the rest of the way off.

As he drew me back into his arms, I turned so my back was pressed against him, giving his hands freedom to roam my breasts, my hips, my thighs. Now I was warm in his embrace while he left soft, warm, moist kisses in the crook of my neck.

"Nina, you're driving me crazy," he whispered in my ear, sending shivers all over my skin.

"I want you inside me, Max," I said, just dreaming of that thick cock sliding into me.

Max groaned and squeezed my breasts full in his palms, rolling and massaging them. My nipples protruded between his fingers and he pinched them, making me gently moan and rock my buttocks against his cock. I felt it bobbing eagerly against my cheeks, and instinctively I began to roll my hips and let the tip prod my outer labia.

There would be no time for extended foreplay. I wanted him – no, *needed him* – right now.

I angled my hips so that my juicy labia kissed the head of his cock, giving him the invitation to slide inside me. Max's warm hand found my thigh and lifted it, holding my left breast firm in his other hand.

"Are you sure you want it?" he asked, his voice thick and ragged with his heavy breathing.

"God, yes," I said, lifting my thigh a little higher to open myself for him.

"You're a beautiful goddess," he said into my ear, kissing my lobe. "You've enchanted me since the second I met you. I've fantasised about this very moment, but I never thought..."

Max let his left hand leave my breast and reached down to dab two fingers on my clit. I was so small in his arms that I fit perfectly, allowing him to reach my aching little nub. As his fingers rolled my clit inside its hood, I cried out loud, almost climaxing under his firm, confident touch. Max sent pulses of pleasure up throughout the walls of my vagina and deep inside my womb as he prodded and gently pulled, fucking my clit with his fingertips. I couldn't hold myself off from grinding against them, wanting more, loving every pulse and throb of pleasure.

The only thing that could really send me to heaven would be his large, throbbing cock stuffing me full, giving me something hard to ride while I climaxed.

"Max, fuck me," I begged breathlessly.

His fingertips only made firmer, tiny circular motions as he rolled my clit and pressed it intermittently.

"You're going to make me come, beautiful," he said against my neck, kissing me sloppily with loose, warm lips. "Are you ready?"

"Oh god, Max, yes," I said, turning my face into his thick, flexing bicep.

He pressed my clitoris in, firmly, as he angled his cock and thrust. I groaned against his arm as his cock head popped open my passage and made way for his thickness, stretching me to capacity and stuffing me full. His erection slid inside me to the very hilt, the head of his cock only stopping as it nudged my cervix.

"Fuck, you're tight," he said, still holding up my leg in one hand, as if it weighed nothing. "God, Nina, just the ridges inside you have brought me to the edge. If you so much as moved – "

I held still as long as I could, but the moment his fingertips worked my clit again, I was climbing and climbing at a pace so rapid that I began to cry out and wail.

"I can't hold back Max –"

"Come for me," Max said into my ear, as he jerked his cock and pumped me hard, giving me something to really *come* on. I reached my peak and climaxed, orgasming against the stiff column of his cock. The pulses of my vaginal walls were sated against his firm plug. As I bounced against him he groaned out loud, suddenly thrusting much harder, faster.

"Nina, Nina," he panted, slamming his cock up toward the opening of my womb. I felt him go rock solid as he shattered inside me, crying out my name with every stroke of climax. His face was burrowed inside the crook of my neck as his seed shot up inside me, coating my insides in his smooth, balmy load. I moved my pelvis up and down gently as his cock pulsed, enjoying the feeling of every spurt, knowing it was all for me.

He sighed and nuzzled my neck, wrapping his arms tightly around my body. I was entirely weakened by my orgasm, my clit still throbbing. Max turned me and bundled me against his hard, warm body. We pressed our lips together and sank into another deep, delicious kiss. His arms felt so right around me that I didn't want the moment to end, and he didn't seem to, either.

In fact, we drew out the process as long as possible. Max lowered his head and suckled my nipples until I was bucking against him in pleasure, and his sated cock returned once again to a long, stiff, rod. He took me again – laying on top of me and jerking so hard the bed creaked – and once more with me in his lap, his back against my headboard. From that angle we were able to tongue one another's wanting mouths and cry out our orgasms in unison. His warm hands cupped my buttocks and spanked me as I came.

Max was heaven in the sack; absolute bliss.

And I knew it couldn't last.

I was due to fly out to Kampala, Uganda, in just two weeks' time.

As Max cradled me in his arms and kissed me a final time, I couldn't know that his sperm would be competing their way up to meet my waiting egg.

As a very busy woman who – until that moment – wasn't getting any in the sack, I didn't even remember that I'd missed several of my birth control pills that month. With all the excitement that followed of packing, preparing, and leaving instructions for the woman sitting my apartment, I didn't even notice when I missed my period. Eventually I assumed with all the stress of the move, they'd temporarily stopped. It wouldn't have been the first time.

I boarded the plane feeling optimistic for my next two years' residency in the World International Hospital, where I would be serving my secondment. What I didn't know was that a whole universe was attaching itself to the lining of my womb, where its cells would divide and grow.

Five months later, I collapsed with exhaustion after a difficult shift involving the loss of several patients. Run off my feet in a permanently warm environment, the last thing I expected to learn was that I was 20 weeks pregnant.

As I watched my womb expand and grow, I thought almost constantly about Max – remembering his words about never wanting children, and how it was a sore spot for him given that it played a part in ending his marriage. More than a few times, in my third trimester, I thought of calling him. But I just couldn't. He hadn't banked on a baby any more than I had, and besides – what if he flat-out rejected them?

I couldn't risk impacting Max and his career, and I couldn't risk the rejection of what would turn out to be the happiest surprise of all my life. To think that he might deem our daughter unwelcome in this world was just unthinkable.

It would be better, I decided, to raise her myself and ensure she only knew love and support. Besides, I still had the rest of my secondment to finish – and with the help of the on-site nursery, I got back on the horse 10 weeks after her birth, still close enough to tend to my daughter and breast-feed her.

It was only when I was planning our flights back to London that my gut started churning with anxiety, knowing that I would be carrying a big secret on board.

That secret's name was Maxina; a blend of my name, and her father's.

# CHAPTER FOUR
♥

*Max*

As Dr Bellamy and Dr Hurst jointly raised a toast to me and my engagement to Hannah Shepherd, LA plastic surgeon to the stars, the door to the break room opened and was very gently closed. Somebody was late to our little mid-shift get together.

The last person I expected to see was Nina Dorrington, my ex-colleague and by far one of the greatest spontaneous sexual experiences of my life. I daren't think it, but I couldn't help it: all right, *the* best sexual experience.

But there she was, with a healthy tan and her blonde hair streaked with white, bleached presumably from the sun. She looked so good, even better than I remembered her two years ago before she left for Kampala.

My eyes couldn't help but drift to her as my colleagues applauded and I took a long sip of faux-champagne. It couldn't have been more inappropriate of me to think this, but I couldn't stop myself – images of her divine little body opened up in my mind like a blooming flower. Her full, perfect breasts, the face she pulled when she was thrown into another orgasm; the way her chest flushed pink when she climaxed.

It all flooded back as I swallowed my celebration faux-champagne, toasting my fiancé who was away on work in the states. I should have felt guilty, but I only felt...drawn. Drawn to her.

"I couldn't think of a better union than between you and Hannah Shepherd," said Dr Bellamy, raising his glass up high.

"We're happy for you, sir," said Dr Hurst, taking a sip of her champagne. "You had to tie the knot sometime."

"The only question is – whose name will you both be taking? You're both world-renowned surgeons in the top of your respective fields," said Dr Bellamy.

"Er, we er – " My eyes followed the small blonde Nina as she moved among the back row with her head bowed, hiding behind a curtain of hair. Pulling my gaze away was torture – for some bizarre reason – but I forced myself before anybody noticed. Fuck, *why* did she have to come back now, of all times? Why now, when I had just announced my engagement?

"Max?"

They were waiting, their eyes searching among the crowd of nurses, admin staff, and residents to see what had caught my eye.

"We're thinking of keeping our own names," I mumbled, realising that they had followed my transfixed gaze and spotted her too.

"Look who's here!" said Dr Hurst. "Just in time to give you her congratulations! Nina, come and grab a glass and celebrate."

She was avoiding me; I could see that. No wonder, too. She had to be thinking the same thing I was – that this was just my bastard luck to make an announcement like this when she was due to return. Well, sod it – we'd have to make it work. It was just a fling, after all – a memorable one, all right, but it was over as quickly as it began. A couple weeks later and she flew away out of my life. I'd wished her well.

Hannah was dynamite in bed, had legs for days, and she appreciated my work. As a certified star of cosmetic and re-constructive surgery, it had bowled me over to be recognised for my work with neonates by her of all people. We'd hit if off instantly during her visit here at Sacred Heart, our minds meeting as well as our bodies, and it all fell quickly into place. We'd flown Hannah in to offer cosmetic surgery on some of our patients with various issues, from burns to deformations. Just six months later, here we were – or here I was, anyway – announcing our plans to wed.

Together we were going to be an unstoppable force, especially when we moved to the USA after the wedding. In California, she said, I'd practically be a rock star. There'd be a chance to make a real difference in their central children's hospital and make a shit-ton of money while I was at it.

What wasn't there to love about that? It had been my ambition since childhood to do just that.

I only had to wait for my work VISA application to go through and then, after saying our vows and signing a bit of paper, we could jet off into the sunset – my superstar surgeon bride, and me, the superstar surgeon groom. All right, maybe it sounded a bit too perfect to be true – but for a working class kid from up north, it was all I'd ever dreamed of and more.

Yet I could feel Nina's eyes on me, now; I could sense her somewhere in the room. It was a crazy thing to think, yet every part of me was reacting; even my skin had goose-flesh, just thinking of Nina being there in the same room as me. Like an irritation, the moment I saw her, the feelings only grew. She was niggling away at me, urging me to just scratch that itch.

I only wish I understood why. She was just a colleague I slept with, wasn't she? Heck, she wasn't even the first, though I wasn't proud of that fact. It was hardly in-keeping with the rules for senior surgeons to copulate with their own team members, but I was a single man with very little time to fraternize outside of the workplace.

Bugger it – I regretted nothing. If Nina found it

too hard to look me in the eye and wanted to skulk around trying to avoid me now, then let her. I had a job to get on with. I found myself scowling in her direction, anticipating her rejection of me when she lifted her head and met my eyes with hers; the dark, mystical irises were just as I remembered them, drawing me in. Nina had always looked as though she had some psychic insight, like she knew something I didn't; and beside her, I felt like an ogre towering over a magical priestess. I had all the brawn, but she wielded the real power.

Why the hell did she *still* make me feel like that? I could feel it now, even after two years. It was no use; I couldn't stand the agitation anymore. As the staff mingled, I bullied my way between them and shot out a hand in greeting to Nina, who flinched as if a wasp had just stung her. She took my hand abruptly, as if only just waking up from a trance and seeing it there.

"Max," she said.

"Nina. You sound like you were expecting someone else."

"Of course not," she said. "I'm sorry. I saw you and I – I was just thinking."

I guided Nina over to where the non-alcoholic champagne bottle stood on the break-room coffee station and poured her a glass. There was barely more than a dribble left, but it was a mouthful.

She raised the glass, though not quite catching my eye, and mumbled, "Cheers" as she took a sip. She grimaced as it went down as if she was swallowing petrol.

"Well, don't look too enthusiastic," I said.

"It's been a while since I've drunk anything alcoholic. I've been brea – " she stopped short suddenly, her eyes widening. Then she frowned and shook her head, as if admonishing herself.

"Nina?"

"Huh? S-sorry, Max, ignore me. I'm still, er – I'm still on Kampala time," she said. "It's going to take a little while for me to adjust. Everything looks to be just as I left it. Well, except you, I suppose..."

"What's different about me? And by the way – that drink tastes like arse because it's non-alcoholic, not real champagne. We're on the clock after all."

She cocked an eyebrow, looking me square in the face now. Her tan had brought out hundreds of tiny brown freckles that I'd never seen before. I found myself entranced by them, until I realised I was staring.

"Max?"

"W-what? Yes, I said – what's different about me?"

She blinked. "And I answered: you're engaged now. Engaged people look different somehow. They have a little...I don't know, a glow, I guess."

"A glow?" I asked in a flat tone of voice. "Do I really look like I've got a poxy glow?"

She smiled, then, looking slightly more relaxed. "Your own particular kind of glow, I suppose, yes," she said.

It was her who was glowing from all the sunshine and travel, but I couldn't say that. It felt wrong to even think it, let alone mention it. I was an engaged man now. It wasn't a state that I felt suited me; like an oddly fitting shirt that I'd have to get used to wearing. If I was honest with myself, this whole nonsense with the celebration was giving me hives, but I went along with it for the sake of team spirit. Hannah wasn't even in the country, for Christ's sake – what sort of engagement party involved only the groom?

"Max?"

I shook my head free of all those negative thoughts. Thinking that way never got anybody anywhere.

"You, er – you look good, Nina. All that warm weather and Ugandan spirit has clearly done you wonders," I said, resuming my usual, more authoritative tone. "You can tell me all about it while I give you a tour, if you like."

"Oh? I get a tour, now?"

"Of course," I said. "All part of the service."

I took her to nursery room three first, making our way up from there to the most critical unit. We started at the nursing station and walked side-by-side along the corridor.

"These are the bins, orange and black – you

may remember those from two years ago," I said. "Here's the nursing station with the shitty old computers and the system that needed updating ten years ago."

Nina covered her mouth and snorted with laughter, realising, as I intended to show her, that absolutely bugger all had changed in the 24 months since she'd been away.

"Here we have the cleaning cupboard, with the colour-coded mop heads that always get mixed up regardless of the hygiene system. Here's the sluice room – still stinks of baby pee, but don't let that put you off. You'll be a great asset to the team here."

"Hey, that's a good smell – it means all their plumbing is functioning as it should be," said Nina, digging me in the ribs with her elbow. Why did my heart do a little back-flip when she nudged me? Since *when* did I react like that to anyone?

"Couldn't agree more," I said, moving us toward nursery room two. "So what did you get up to over there?"

"All sorts – it was amazing, really. I became really familiar with obstetrics and helped deliver a lot of babies, then got to follow through with their care afterwards. It was truly eye-opening. One of the best decisions I ever made," she said, frowning as she said it.

"What's the face for?"

"Huh? Oh, nothing – I was just thinking, we've both been busy, that's all. It's amazing how life can take such a sudden turn – different to how you expected."

"Right," I said, feeling baffled about what the hell she was getting at now. "And I suppose you got stuck in as soon as you got there, eh? I bet they kept you busy."

"Absolutely," she said, blowing out her cheeks. "It was really difficult when I was put out of action, but I soon got on my feet."

"Out of action? What happened?"

She bit her lip, as if wanting to say something and deciding against it. She wiped her brow. Was it hot on the ward? I hadn't noticed.

"I caught a common bug they have over there. It, uh – I was a patient for a few weeks, but I bounced back."

"I see," I said. "Well, I'm glad to hear it."

We stopped by the bunk rooms where staff could grab a little shut-eye if they needed to, or if they needed a place to decompress. Being in such close proximity to the beds brought thoughts into my mind of that morning after the heavy rain, when I'd drawn Nina into my arms, in her own bed, and everything had somehow felt right.

I swatted the thought away like a buzzing fly. I didn't need thoughts like that distracting me now that I was engaged.

"Anyway, what about you? Engaged, huh? I never thought I'd see the day. Who proposed?" Nina cocked her head to one side, looking genuinely intrigued – I thought I'd better answer her, even though it made me feel oddly uncomfortable to do so.

"Actually we just…came to an agreement over dinner one evening," I said. "We bought the ring together."

Nina raised her eyebrows. "So she's not the overly romantic type who expected you to get down on one knee on Tower Bridge then, no?"

I chuckled. "No, absolutely not. Hannah's definitely unique in that respect. She said she hated anything corny, so we uh…we did it her way. I wasn't fussed either way," I said.

Now Nina looked confused. I couldn't imagine why – it wasn't that difficult to understand. We'd decided to get married, and that was it – why the need for all the fluff, anyway?

"So, how long had you been seeing each other?" she asked.

I wasn't sure of the relevance, but I answered her anyway.

"Less than six months," I said. "Why?"

Nina shrugged. "I just thought that's the sort of perfunctory way of couples that have known each other for years and years and don't have anything to prove…I would have thought at six months you'd be in the honeymoon phase, all saccharine and – "

"We're not all about candles and sodding roses, Nina." I snapped, making her flinch. I regretted it instantly, but I felt anger brewing in my head and I couldn't help myself. What business was it of hers, anyway? "Some of us are professionals."

"Woah, pipe down," she said, looking perplexed and irritated. "It was just an observation."

"You're not here to observe me, Nina. Since when did you care about the intricacies of my love-life? I've not heard owt from you since your plane took off," I said, folding my arms across my chest.

Nina looked down at her feet, the uneasy look returning to her. "Did that bother you? Not hearing from me?"

I sniffed, looking away at my colleagues busying themselves between rooms, getting back to it. "Of course not," I said, knowing I was lying. "But it hardly entitles you to pry into my life the minute you see me again."

"Point taken," she said, breathing out a long sigh. "Listen, Max, whenever you get a minute free, I think there's something you – "

The alarm blared, making us both jump. The light above nursery room one was flashing.

"All hands on deck, people! Let's move it!" I bellowed. "You ready, Nina?"

"You bet," she said, taking off and running. I sprinted up the hall after her, unwrapping my stethoscope as I went.

# CHAPTER FIVE
♥

*Nina*

"She was fine one minute, and the next she was turning blue," said baby Amy's startled mother, looking white as a sheet herself. "I don't know what happened. What's happening to my baby?"

"Get mum out of here, Nina," said Max as he pressed his stethoscope to the baby's chest and examined the sats monitor, his eyes scanning it rapidly.

I put my arm around the baby's mother and hurried her out of the room, assuring her that the doctors would do everything they possibly could. Bundling her into the break room with two of my HCA colleagues – who had calmed the nerves of more parents than you could fit inside an airplane hangar – I sprinted back to nursery room one.

Dr Bellamy and Dr Hurst had joined Max by this point; they were a jumble of elbows and plastic tubes, with Max barking orders at them. They were intubating the baby, who was struggling to draw in enough oxygen to circulate around her tiny body.

"I've got it!" I shouted, assisting Dr Hurst. I held the baby's airway open while Dr Hurst threaded the tube into her trachea. Dr Bellamy provided a source of light and supervised her positioning.

"It's too big," said Dr Hurst, her voice wavering in agitation. "Get me a size down, Nina."

I rummaged in the drawers crammed with plastic tubing until I found a 2.5. I took deep breaths, trying to keep my cool against the sounds of the machine bleeping rapidly.

"76 percent and dropping," said Max in a clipped tone. "Get that tubing, Nina."

"I've got it," I said, feeding it to Dr Hurst. She blew a strand of hair out of her face as she swapped over, tossing the useless tubing aside.

"72 percent."

"Fucking hell, I need more light." Dr Hurst glared at Dr Bellamy, who angled his pen light closer and pressed two fingers to the baby's neck.

I tipped her head back, opening her as wide as I could. She was tiny, fragile, still pink and barely at full-term. I'd learned in our morning brief that she was three weeks premature with congestion and breathing difficulties, but otherwise presented normally. She had been expected to do well, but had deteriorated over the course of the morning before turning this alarming shade of pale blue-grey.

"I see chords," said Dr Hurst, threading it down.

"There. Nurse, administer puffs."

I took over with the baby's breathing, administering gentle puffs of air. The sats machine blipped, her oxygen saturations rising gradually.

"Good, good. Nice work, Dr Hurst," said Max. "I need her most recent X-ray and ultrasound scans. Hurst? Bellamy?"

Dr Bellamy shared an uneasy glance with Dr Hurst. "Obstetrics decided we didn't need them, Max. Her EKG came back okay. She's on monitoring."

"Well that worked out bloody well, didn't it?" said Max, flushing red.

I hadn't been around him for long, yet I could see he'd changed over the last couple of years. He seemed to be twice as stressed as I recalled him ever looking before, as if permanently on-edge and ready to snap.

He certainly wasn't acting in accordance with a man who was in love and recently engaged, but then again – this was Sacred Heart Children's Hospital, and this was Max Hartcliffe. I should hardly be surprised.

"She presented well – don't blame obstetrics," said Dr Hurst.

"This isn't about blame, this is about doing the appropriate tests and gathering the right information!" Max bellowed. "I want a bedside echocardiogram, X-ray, the works – Nina, get me another EKG. Dr Hurst can take over. Get obstetrics in here – I want to know exactly what they've done so far."

Dr Hurst took over the puffs, balancing it gently above the baby's head. Her colour was improving, but not quickly enough. They would get her hooked up to oxygen once she was stable enough.

"82 percent and climbing," said Dr Bellamy. "Nina – it was Javindha in the central delivery suite. Drag her back from lunch if you have to – just get her here."

"I don't care if you have to drag her back from a dentist's chair – get her here pronto," said Max, in a grumbling voice that told me he was not messing about, and would make heads roll if he had to.

"Got it."

I ran from the room, knowing already what Max was thinking – that this was a possible VSD: a ventricular septal defect, or hole in the heart. He would need evidence to support his suspicions before they could run further tests. In the meantime, the baby would be high-risk and would need very close, careful monitoring. My own heart was telling me that within the next couple of hours, I would be breaking the news to baby Amy's terrified mother that her daughter had a congenital heart defect, and would need surgery right away.

♥

The tests confirmed Max's hunch – Amy did have a heart defect. I brought Max in to meet her mother and explain her options, which were really down to two: allow time and monitoring to see if the defect could self-repair as Amy grew, or perform surgery.

"Mrs Thompson, I strongly advise that you allow me to perform surgery. My scans are showing a serious defect, and in my experience defects like this – at this size, this magnitude – don't heal themselves. I'd be putting Amy at serious risk if we left it to chance now," said Max, showing Amy's bewildered mother the scans depicting exactly where the leak was occurring.

"But what if you do more harm than good?" she asked, tears streaming down her face. "What if it's better to wait?"

"That's something we can do," said Max. "But in my experience it's better to act now than to allow it time to do further damage. It's a large defect we're dealing with – I think we'd be rushing her into surgery before the day is out."

I glanced at Max, wishing he'd make some attempt to be more tactful – the poor woman was scared enough. But it wasn't his job to sugar-coat anything, and the facts were the facts – I knew he had to be clear to give Mrs Thompson the best chance of understanding what was going to happen with her daughter.

Mrs Thompson wiped her tear-streaked face with a shaking hand. "All right. Do what you need to do to make her better," she said.

Max and I shared a long sigh of relief as we made our way back to Amy's cot-side. Mrs Thompson would get a moment to kiss Amy and stroke her before we wheeled her away. It was a moment that I never failed to find painful – especially when I thought of my own baby, Maxina, and how I'd feel if it were her laying there.

Since becoming a mother, my work-life experience hadn't been the same again, and never would be. I fought hard against the urge to see my own child in every baby we treated in Kampala, and I knew I'd have the same problem here in the UK. Everything – and I mean everything – had been easier before I became a mother. Less complicated, less tiring, less heart-wrenching.

And yet just as I knew Mrs Thompson wouldn't ever regret Amy, even for all the worry and heartache she'd caused since her birth, I would never, ever regret my beautiful daughter.

Max looked up from his notes on Amy with a twinkle in his blue-green eyes. A shiver ran over me, making my blood run cold, as I recognised Maxina's eyes in him – she'd inherited her father's colour, like the sparkling Mediterranean sea on a sunny day. Those were eyes that I loved and cherished, and there they were on the face of the man standing before me.

"Well?"

I blinked. "Wait, you want me to scrub-in?"

"Of course," he said. "Let's get you back with a

bang. Unless you think you can't handle it?"

I swallowed hard, my heart beating fast. "Of course I can damn-well handle it," I said, storming after him as he led the way to theatre.

♥

The surgery was supposed to take around two hours, but it ended up taking twice that, at least. Amy was hooked up to a heart-lung bypass machine, allowing for Max to make the necessary repairs while the machine breathed for her. While I assisted Max with opening up Amy's tiny chest cavity and passing him the necessary equipment, Dr Ravi, neonatal anaesthesiologist, kept her stable and sedated.

Dr Hurst and Dr Bellamy worked either side of the table to open the tiny cavity and provide assistance with cauterising. I sucked in a breath behind my mask. There, in the centre-left, was Amy's tiny beating heart; a muscle so strong that it kept going in spite of the tear that threatened to end her life, and would be stopped temporarily while Max made his repairs. His hands worked delicately, efficiently, making slight movements as he gazed deeply through his magnifying glasses.

"Fuck, stem it – Hurst, stem it now before we have a problem," said Max.

"Got it," said Dr Hurst as a sudden spray of blood shot up from Amy's chest cavity.

Even after all these years, I still couldn't believe what I was seeing; my body was flooded with adrenaline and endorphins to see them working, and to be a part of it.

"And there it is, you little beauty," said Max, locating the defect. "I'm going to patch her up now."

Max's eyes glowed as he concentrated, his movements so slight and deliberate that he looked as though he had practised operating on mice.

Amy's breast would forever bear the scar of her early surgery, but she would be a child who could run, dance, play sports – and, with all being well, would never experience weakness of the heart again. As Dr Hurst and Dr Bellamy closed, Max and I left to dispose of our scrubs and get a shower. It had been a successful surgery, and Max was upbeat, positively radiating with energy. That was the Max I remembered, and I was relieved to see that he was still there, underneath all the tension I'd observed in him earlier.

I left Max to give Mrs Thompson the good news. As I took a towel from my locker, the changing room door opened and closed. Max's hand was on my shoulder, giving it a squeeze.

"Good work in there, Nina. I'm impressed that you could get your head in the game so quickly."

"Of course," I said. "It's what I do."

"I know, I know," said Max, tossing a bottle of water between his hands. "It's just we never got the chance to work together like that again before you left. I always thought that was a shame."

"Oh?" I asked. "And what made you think that'd be a good idea?"

Max smirked, but I thought I detected a blushing behind his stubble. "I asked around after you, when you left. I was hoping we'd get the chance to work together in the operating room and really get a feel for each other again as colleagues, instead of just...well – "

"Say no more," I said. "You're almost a married man now."

"Right, right," said Max, tossing the water bottle. "We don't need to go over old ground."

I paused, an awful gut-wrenching feeling passing through me. If only he knew just *how much* ground we in fact had to go over.

"Actually, Max, about that...there is something I wanted to – "

An obnoxious vibrating sound cut me off. Max blinked as if unsure where the noise came from. Then suddenly he remembered, and pulled his phone from his pocket.

"Ah, I'm sorry, Nina. It's Hannah. Do you mind if I take this?"

I gulped, folding the towel against my belly, wishing I could use it to squash the awful feeling churning away inside me.

"Er – I don't know if – "

"She's calling from the states," said Max, his thumb hovering over the green answer button.

"Unless it's important?"

"Of c-course not. G-god, no," I said, stuttering. "I need to get showered and get back to it, anyway."

"Thanks, Nina – and thanks again for today," said Max, slipping out of the room as he answered the call.

I ran for the toilet, slamming the door shut behind me.

I barely had time to flip up the toilet seat before I vomited. It was impossible – utterly impossible. *How would I ever dig my way out of this,* I asked myself. This wasn't just a secret I was hiding – it was a bomb, a weapon of mass destruction. Maxina, our love-child, had the ability to destroy Max's new engagement. Who knew what else she could do? Just the knowledge of her existence could have a ripple effect, and who knew how far that would spread?

Our daughter was in a nursery, entirely unaware of how much disaster her existence could cause. And it was all my fault. While we were in Uganda together, it had felt like another world entirely – but now that we were home, it had suddenly become very, very real.

I would have to tread lightly in the meantime, and keep my secret close. The thought of wiping that proud smile off of Max's face as he realised I was not the reliable, dependable nurse he thought I was – well, it gave me palpitations. I showered, hoping if I just scrubbed hard enough, I could wash off all the guilt and let it spiral away down the plug-hole.

# CHAPTER SIX

♥

*Max*

"Mrs Thompson, Amy has been consistently improving since her surgery. I'm delighted to say that if she keeps this up, you'll be taking her home within the next couple of weeks," I said, enjoying the thrill of what was one of my favourite parts of the job – bragging about our successes. The elated smiles on the faces of the parents made every critical, stressful moment in the OR completely worthwhile. That, and, of course – the knowledge that Amy's quality of life will have been dramatically improved for our intervention.

When I saw the sparks of hope glittering in Mrs Thompson's eyes, I remembered why I wanted to be a surgeon.

"I can't thank you enough, doctor. You spotted the problem when the obstetric team thought it was nothing more than a little congestion," said Mrs Thompson.

"These things happen," I said. "Sometimes it just takes a second look, a fresh pair of eyes. I'm just glad we found the defect sooner rather than later."

I continued my morning ward rounds with a good feeling in my gut; it was going to be a beautiful day. Looking outside at the cityscape beyond the window, I could see it was in fact another drizzling February morning with typical British weather – wasn't it always pissing it down? But in my ward, things were looking up.

My only issue was that I hadn't spoken to Hannah properly in three days. She was knee-deep in nose jobs and breast enlargements, and she had very little time for me. I respected that, just as she respected my work – it was one of the reasons we agreed to get married. It just made sense for us to be that couple and, besides, I was over the moon with excitement when I thought of all the critical care I could provide to the neonates in Los Angeles.

As I checked my notes and made my way down the corridor toward the next nursery, an uneasy feeling throbbed in my belly. There was something I was nervous about when I thought about moving to Los Angeles, but I couldn't quite put my finger on what. It was a gut-wrenching feeling, as if I felt homesick before I'd even gotten on a plane, knowing I would likely never return.

What about the kids in the UK who needed to be operated on? Wasn't I depriving them of my skills?

"Don't be daft." I grumbled to myself under my breath.

There were many well-capable surgeons in the

UK who would ensure those lives were in the very best hands – and two of them worked with me. Dr Hurst and Dr Bellamy may not have reached my level of experience yet, but they were fast getting there. Who was I to assume they'd need me here forever?

"Now get over yourself you arrogant sod," I said, pushing open the door to nursery room two. Dr Hurst was observing a newcomer to the ward.

"Max, meet Tabby, born at 32 weeks gestation in the girls bathroom of a local high school," said Dr Hurst, moving the stethoscope around Tabby's chest.

"Holy hell," I said, shaking my head. "How are the parents?"

"She's pretending to be shocked, but her head of year suspects she was well-aware of the pregnancy, and was trying to hide it," said Dr Hurst.

"I meant the girl's parents – the grandparents to this child," I said.

"Oh. Well, I guess the mother didn't feel she could be honest with them," said Dr Hurst. "It happens."

"You mean there was a baby on the way and the girl's parents had no idea their daughter was pregnant until she gave birth in a toilet stall?"

I couldn't get my head around that. I'd been lucky enough to be close to my parents, with a good amount of trust between us. All right, my dad was a bit of a bastard with an anger problem, and we butted heads, but I couldn't imagine keeping a secret of that scale from them.

Dr Hurst shrugged. "I know that if I'd been a pregnant teenager, I would *never* have been able to tell my parents. Who knows – maybe I'd be giving birth in the girls' room too."

"Who's the father? Does he know?"

Dr Hurst sighed. "She's keeping her lips sealed on that, too. Apparently she's too terrified to admit who it is just yet. We can only hope there wasn't any grooming or abuse involved."

I turned and paced the room, my chest feeling tight. Sorrow came over me for the young girl who had to face something so traumatic all alone, and for the baby who would be raised in a world of confusion by a mother too young to know what to do for the best – to the point where she'd hidden the pregnancy entirely.

"How old is the mother?" I asked, knowing I wasn't going to find the answer easy to hear.

"She's fourteen," said Dr Hurst.

"Bloody hell," I said, trying to suppress my own feelings of anger that were rising inside me. "She's just a baby herself."

"It's just one of those things," said Dr Hurst.

"I want to knock these kids' heads together," I said, hoping it was more of a Romeo and Juliet scenario, and not anything more serious - like somebody much older impregnating a young girl.

"How is the baby doing?"

"She's doing remarkably well," said Dr Hurst. "She's strong, she's coping. She just needs a little assistance with oxygen, and other than that it's regular milk feeds until she's strong enough to take a bottle."

"Good, good," I said. "Keep me posted on her progress. When's the mother coming down?"

"She needed some stitching, the poor lamb, but they're going to wheel her in when she's done in obstetrics," said Dr Hurst. "I've assigned Nina Dorrington to Tabby and the mother – she's so good with children, I figured she'd be perfect."

"Right, because of all her experience abroad, when she worked in midwifery and obstetrics," I said, nodding my agreement. It made sense. She would have worked with mothers of all ages, as well as their children.

I could imagine Nina knowing exactly what to say to Tabby's mother to keep her calm and reassured – I'd be a bull in a china shop, asking the kid what the hell had happened, until she was too terrified to even speak to me. Tact was certainly not my strong point.

But I was working on it.

"Yeah, absolutely – plus because she's got a kid of her own," said Dr Hurst. She adjusted the fluid drip and noted it on Tabby's sheet.

"Pardon? She's got what?"

Dr Hurst looked up from her notes, her blue eyes

looking at me pityingly. "She didn't tell you? Yeah, she's got a little kid at home. Spends a fortune on nursery fees, but I think her mother helps her out too. How she's working like she does with a baby to take care of, I'll never know."

Fury built inside me like a fireball. Nina had brought a child of her own into the world while she was away, and she'd never even mentioned it to me?

"Why the hell didn't she let me know?" I said, pacing the room like an agitated tiger. "We've got the bloody crèche scheme, haven't we? She's wasting all her wages on a nursery?"

"Maybe she wasn't aware of it," said Dr Hurst.

"She'd have been made aware of every single benefit known to man if she had chuffing-well told me that she had an infant," I bellowed, making Dr Hurst hush me as she tended the baby. "I'm sorry. I just – it just pisses me off when my staff don't tell me things. How I can help if they don't let me?"

Dr Hurst raised an eyebrow at me. "Maybe she thought you'd go volcanic on her like you are right now, sir."

I grunted. "Why would she possibly think that? Shouldn't she have at least tried first before making that assumption?"

"Sir," said Dr Hurst, sighing as she put her hands on her hips. "Nobody dares to upset you. You have a way of making them regret asking for help."

"Bollocks," I said, hearing Dr Hurst chuckle as

I turned away from her. She was right – I knew deep down she was right. Nina was probably embarrassed to be coming back to work with a dependant she hadn't – as far as I could tell, anyway – planned on, and she didn't know how to ask for support.

But there was support on offer, and I was going to damn-well make sure she got it. She was spending thousands of pounds on nursery fees when she could be making use of the hospital crèche and paying less than a third of that with her staff benefit.

"The stupid bloody woman," I said under my breath as I left the room in search of Nina. I felt like I wanted to give her a good shake by the shoulders. I couldn't understand why I felt so explosive about it; my head was so full of rage. I just couldn't understand it. Why would she want to punish herself just because she was afraid of me? I thought we had an understanding, me and her. We'd looked out for each other two years ago, hadn't we?

What had changed?

I stopped outside the feeding suite where I knew Nina was giving support to parents via video link – mostly mothers who needed to understand peg-feeding and supplying breast milk to babies who weren't able to ingest it normally. As I waited, hearing her voice behind the door, my heart softened and guilt fell over me like a burst of rain.

That was it – that was why I felt so angry. It was the thought of Nina suffering because she couldn't come to me. The thought of her working so bloody hard and not seeing a penny of her wages, while she missed time with her child. She could see them any time she wanted in the Sacred Heart staff crèche. It made me furious.

With myself.

# CHAPTER SEVEN
♥

*Nina*

I ended the video-link feeling bright and airy, knowing I had delivered some good advice to the parents at home with babies who had left our care. It was a great feeling, when parents asked lots of questions and I found myself able to answer them fluidly. Every piece of good feeding advice shared would directly benefit the baby, and would give the parents peace of mind too. I sighed a happy sigh as I packed away my example pegs and syringes for demonstrations, thinking about how good it felt to be home again, doing what I loved in my own hospital.

If only I wasn't hiding a whopping great secret, maybe I could have enjoyed that feeling. But my body didn't allow me to feel any joy for long; not when Maxina's father was still completely in the dark about who she was and, more pressingly, who *he* was.

The door opened – it was Dr Hurst, poking her head around the door. "Nina – you're in nursery room two today with Tabby, our new arrival. 32 weeks gestation."

"Perfect," I said, zipping up my bag. "What's her story?"

Dr Hurst carefully slipped into the room and closed the door behind her. "The mother is just fourteen – she's due to come up to the ward soon and be with Tabby. She gave birth in the bathroom stall at school."

I gasped, feeling the magnitude of the situation – the secrets, the lies. The fear that poor girl must have been experiencing, never mind the agony.

"Holy hell. Mother and baby are okay?"

"She's peachy – just needs general care for her prematurity. Actually, it's the mother I wanted to assign you to – I have a feeling you'll be good for her," said Dr Hurst. "She needs kindness and a soft voice, and she's hardly going to get that from Max."

I rolled my eyes. "Of course not. He's about as graceful as a Bison in a tutu about these things. All right, leave them with me."

"I knew I could count on you," said Dr Hurst. "Oh, and uh – watch out for Max. He's on a bit of a rampage today."

Dr Hurst slipped back out of the room, leaving me blinking in surprise. What could have wound Max up this early in the shift, when we didn't have anything complex going on? I left the room carrying my supplies and walked straight into Max's brick-wall chest.

"Woah!" I said, steadying myself.

Max scowled down at me as if I'd trodden on his toes.

"Break room, now. I need a word with you," he said gruffly, not even giving me a chance to respond before he stormed off.

"Yes, sir," I muttered under my breath as I followed. As I closed the break room door behind me, I could see the tension in Max's shoulders. Something was really up. A sick feeling came over me.

"A baby," he said. "A baby, and you didn't tell me?"

I froze, feeling my blood running cold before it drained clean out of me. Weakness filtered into my limbs, right down to my fingertips.

"What do you think you're doing, keeping a secret from me like that?"

My mouth opened but I couldn't speak; couldn't get the words out. Oh god, how had he found out about Maxina? How could he possibly know *he* was the father?

The room tilted and I stumbled, grabbing hold of the table holding our coffee mugs and espresso machine. The scent of the coffee grounds was nauseating.

"Nina? Bloody heck, Nina – what's wrong?" Max grabbed me by the shoulders and guided me to the sofa, taking a heavy seat next to me. The room continued spinning, making me groan. "I didn't mean to bark at you like that. Please, Nina, say something."

"I didn't know how to tell you," I said all in one go, feeling like I might be sick at any moment. "For God's sake Max, *think about it*. How could I tell you when I knew how you'd react?"

I realised then that Max had left his hand on me, and was rubbing the space between my shoulder blades. He seemed to realise himself, then, and drew his hand abruptly away.

"Look, I know I can be a rough bastard, but this is something I needed to know. How else can I support you if you don't tell me these things?"

His voice sounded lighter now, like he was making the effort to be kinder, more reassuring. Well, he was certainly being shockingly reasonable given that he'd just found out about Maxina. I was taken aback by that.

"You're not angry?"

"Of course I am, I'm fucking furious," he said, though his eyes glittered with kindness that betrayed his words. Something wasn't adding up. "With myself, Nina. I should have made you aware of what was on offer, if I only knew about your situation. Why would I be angry with you? I'm frustrated, yes, but angry – no. I'm pissed off that you felt you couldn't come to me."

The penny dropped, and I felt queasy again. He still didn't know Maxina was *his*. Oh god, I thought – why did that make things so much worse?

"I see," was all I could say, and weakly, too.

"How old is she?"

I gulped, my hands shaking. I held them in my lap so that he wouldn't see. Maxina was fourteen months old now, but I didn't want to be too specific. Not yet. Not until I calmed down enough to keep my head on straight.

"Just about a year old," I said.

Max nodded slowly, and I figured I was off the hook – for now.

"You know one of your employee benefits is the use of the crèche. Dr Hurst says you're paying out of pocket for a private nursery?"

I sighed heavily, knowing it had been a stupid decision – but I was scared, and I booked the nursery with the intention of keeping Maxina well out of the picture until I could figure out how to break the news to him. It was costing me half my wage packet, and it didn't even cover all my hours.

"It's costing me the earth," I admitted. "My mother helps out, especially at weekends and when I'm on night shifts. I don't know what I'd do without her."

"Look, I want you to transfer her to the crèche here at Sacred Heart – give yourself a break. You're working hard, Nina. Be a bloody friend to yourself." Max patted me on the shoulder with his heavy, warm hand. "Or at least let me be a friend to you."

"Got it," I said flatly, knowing just what a good

friend *I* made.

Max got up, shaking his head profusely. "All these secrets. If people would just be honest with one another, we could all be on the same bloody page and nobody would have to suffer. Has Jen told you about your new baby?"

I nodded, flexing my fingers. The feeling was coming back to my hands at least.

"Yes, Dr Hurst told me about Tabby. I'm looking forward to meeting her," I said.

"There's another one who kept her baby a secret, and look at the trouble she's in," said Max. "Jennifer reckons you're the perfect one to support her."

I smiled, feeling some warmth returning to my face, though the irony did not escape me. "That's kind of her."

"I agree with her," said Max, catching my eye for a moment. "You are perfect."

The breath caught in my throat as a blush flooded my face and neck. Max looked away suddenly, staring down at his shoes.

"Perfect for looking after those girls, I mean. You're a good nurse," he said, clearing his throat. "Now look, don't keep anything from me again, all right? I'll let the crèche know to expect you – get down there on your lunch break and fill in those forms."

"Got it," I said. "Will do. Thanks, Max."

He nodded briefly and left the room, leaving me

to shake and panic in peace.

♥

They wheeled Tabby's mother in after lunch. I'd spent the hour filling in forms, realising what an idiot I'd been to think that Max wouldn't hear through the grapevine that I'd had a baby. If anything, I'd only made my situation look more suspicious than it would if I'd just been upfront about it: that I had a baby while I was away in Uganda. So why couldn't I just say that?

*You know very well why*, I thought. *Because Max deserves to know the whole truth.*

If only I could figure out how to tell him without destroying our growing work bond, or forcing him to admit that he had no intention of accepting Maxina as his own. How could I ever respect him after that? And he had told me, after all, that he never wanted children – that they were too much work for him, and would get in the way of his career. What else could I expect?

I would have to transfer to another hospital, live in another town. I'd have to tell Maxina that I'd brought her into a world where her father didn't want her. I'd have to see an ugly side of Max that I never wanted to see. Facing all of that when I wanted to be delivering care to my babies at work was just impossible. They needed me, and frankly, I needed them.

If I could just get my head down, it would be best for all involved if I didn't think about it – at least, for now.

When I walked into the nursery and saw Tabby's mother, my belly did a little flip. She was so very young; so pale, and scared. I felt for her immediately.

"Hey," I said. "I'm nurse Dorrington – I'll be looking after Tabby today, and you, if you need anything."

"Hey," she said from Tabby's cot-side. I noticed that she was seated with the cot lowered enough to let her reach in and touch her – with a sterile glove – but she wasn't doing it. She was watching the baby, seemingly in disbelief, with her hands in her lap.

"She's so tiny," was all she said.

"32 weeks," I said, taking a reading of Tabby's blood pressure and noting it down. Next, I took her temperature. She was doing well. "You're both very lucky. The doctor told me that you weren't expecting to give birth?"

The girl's eyes shifted and lowered, looking down at her lap.

"No," she said.

"What's your name?" I pulled a chair over and sat beside her. I let my hand rest on her arm, giving it a reassuring squeeze. "I'm Nina, but you can just call me Nurse if you like."

"Lexie," she said. "I hate my name."

"That's a great name. You picked a great name

for your baby, too."

Lexie's nose twitched as if she'd heard something displeasing. I sensed that she wasn't yet ready to accept the baby as her own.

"What made you choose that name?" I asked.

"Read it in a book," she said. I noticed a tear meandering its way down her cheek. I hadn't realised she was so close to crying.

"What's wrong, Lexie?"

She sniffed, glancing uneasily at the tiny baby in the cot, masked and patched with tape.

"She doesn't feel like she's anything to do with me," said Lexie. "Is that…is that wrong?"

I pressed my lips together in a firm line, thinking it over. "Not in your circumstances, no. It's probably to be expected. Sometimes when we – " I paused, realising this was going to hit very, very close to home. " – when we disassociate – that is, when we push away thoughts that we don't want to have, and don't want to face up to – we create a distance, and that distance only grows. Did you really not know about this baby, Lexie?"

She frowned hard, and I saw by the wrinkles on her young face that she had spent months in torment over this. It was ageing her prematurely; she looked so young on the surface, at first glance, and yet her expressions spoke of pain and anguish that no young person should ever know.

"No," she said firmly. "I didn't know."

I squeezed her arm again, gently. I wasn't going to press the issue. The baby was here now, and their bond was important. It was perfectly plausible that she really didn't know about the pregnancy, or didn't want to know. We were going to have to figure out together how to ensure that Lexie saw Tabby as her daughter, to enable her to care for her. What happened when they went home was anyone's guess – that would be a job for social services.

"You know you can talk to me," I said. "I have a little girl myself. Her name's Maxina. She's just becoming a toddler now, only just learning to walk."

My circumstances didn't seem to faze Lexie at all; she couldn't relate to me just because we were both mothers. Of course she couldn't. Why would she? She was a teen mother – an incredibly young teen mother at that – and she was in hospital with her premature baby. I knew, quite instinctively, that she would be feeling all alone in the world.

"Where's your mum and dad?" I asked.

Lexie shifted in her wheelchair, wincing. Her pain relief for the stitches would be wearing off right about now.

"Dad's not talking to me," she said, almost in a whisper. "Mum doesn't want to look at me."

I looked at Lexie and how pitiful and weak she seemed, knowing that what she needed right now more than anything else was the strength and love of her parents. I couldn't imagine letting Maxina down like this. But, it wasn't about me, and Lexie's parents didn't have to be a thing like me, or act the way I would.

"Hopefully they'll come around," I said, wishing I could say more, but knowing I would be verging on the inappropriate if I were to pry too much. It was a delicate balance. "Do you have anybody else who might want to come and see you, keep you company? You can have visitors for you and the baby while you stay in our parental suites."

"No," she said in a whisper.

I looked at Lexie; really took in her image. She was a plump girl, wearing a long shirt and a jumper over the top, covering every inch of skin. Her hair was long, lank, and dark; she wore glasses and never seemed to want to meet my gaze. I could see, of course, that her self-esteem wasn't the greatest. She carried herself – even in her wheelchair – as if she didn't want to be seen. She seemed intelligent, deep-thinking.

Something about her was niggling at me. Something else was wrong.

"Did your stitching go okay? You seem so uncomfortable," I said.

"I'm okay," she said, wriggling irritably in her seat. Her brow knitted again.

"Lexie?" I touched her arm gently. "I can see what pain relief we can give you, if you like?"

Lexie flinched as my hand touched her arm.

I realised I felt a dampness there that I hadn't detected before. Something was soaking through her shirt and thick woollen jumper. She was gritting her teeth. Without pause, I set about unbuttoning Lexie's cuff and gently rolling her sleeve up.

"Please, don't – it stings," she said, pulling her arm away. A droplet of blood hit the blue linoleum floor.

"What is this? Oh god, Lexie," I said, revealing two gaping gashes in her forearm. They were two among many, many ridges and cuts that had healed and been re-opened over a long period of time. Lexie was a self-harmer.

"Oh sweetheart," I said, my heart sinking. It was so much worse than I thought.

"Please don't tell anybody," said Lexie, the fear evident in her voice. "I didn't mean to do it so bad."

"Wait here," I said. "I'll get Dr Hurst."

"No, no, don't go – "

"It's going to be all right, Lexie. You're going to need sutures."

"I don't know what to do with the baby!" she cried, tears streaming down her face now. "I don't know how to do fucking *anything*. Please."

I bent down to her level and held her hand in mine. It was shaking.

"All you have to do is be here with her, okay? Just be with her. She needs her mummy."

Lexie nodded, though she didn't look at all reassured.

"I'm going to get your arm fixed up and then we're going to talk about this, all right? You're not alone, Lexie. We're here to help you with all of this," I said, knowing there would be a limit to the support we could provide – but when it came to talking, and listening, I could do that for days.

My words finally seemed to reassure her, and she nodded in understanding.

"Okay," she said. "Hurry back."

As I hurried from the room and prayed Dr Hurst was still on the ward, my head was swimming with the gravity of Lexie's situation. She was just a kid herself, with too much responsibility and a premature baby who needed every bit of love she could get. How could a mother provide that much love for a baby, if she had so little love for herself?

I'd made Maxina my priority when I discovered I was pregnant with her. But I was a grown adult, and although she had been a surprise, I was able to take responsibility. I even managed to keep up my job, although it nearly killed me. Lexie was only a child, with still so much to learn – and yet her dark eyes told me she was aged somehow, in all the wrong ways.

I would have to shed some positive light on her, to show her the way out of this mess. Even if I only made a small difference, I resolved that I wouldn't let Lexie or Tabby leave our care without doing that.

But I was one to talk. I had business of my own that I hadn't tended to by a long-shot, and as I found Dr Hurst and ushered her back to the nursery, I felt the word *hypocrite* burning in the centre of my forehead.

Well, what was work for, if it wasn't to provide a string of useful distractions from my own problems?

# CHAPTER EIGHT
♥

*Max*

I tossed my gown, mask, and gloves, heading for the locker rooms. I was in desperate need of a shower. Hannah was due to touch down this evening from Los Angeles, and I was hoping to smell a little better than a teenage boy fresh off the football pitch before she got here.

It had been a difficult surgery; a newborn with a bowel obstruction and a perforation, each very capable of ending an infant's life. It had been a fiddly operation, no part of it running smoothly, or flowing, as I would usually describe it – where I could go off into a deep trance, concentrating solely on my work.

No, this one had been a ball-ache, and I was feeling antsy. If I bumped into Bellamy or Hurst with any ward-related problems before I got my shower, I was liable to blow-up at them. Thankfully, they were long-term friends and colleagues of mine nowadays – though still under my wing – and they'd long since forgiven my poor impulse control. I hoped.

The locker room was in sight. I could almost feel it now; the warm water soothing the muscles in my back, relaxing me from head to toe. They weren't even decent showers – not even power showers – but given that I practically lived on the neonatal ward, they were the closest thing to heaven for me. I wondered if I might even snatch a nap in one of the bunk-beds. Maybe I'd get lucky.

"Excuse me, doctor, we're looking for our daughter?"

I closed my eyes and sighed, changing my expression just in time as I turned to face the two mature-looking parents before me. They looked closer to my age; a man and a woman with stern expressions, quite far from the usual sorrow or joy we saw day-in, day-out from the parents we met on our ward.

"The *teenager*," the man said bitterly, through gritted teeth. As he said those two words, the woman dipped her head, shaking it, as if working through some deep embarrassment. I knew instantly they were Lexie's parents – poor Tabby's grandparents – and I was already getting an idea of the situation here.

"Has she consented to seeing you?" I asked. "I've not been told about any visitors."

The woman looked up abruptly, and the man blinked rapidly as if I'd just slapped him across the chops.

"Of course she consents. We're her parents. She's –" he hushed his voice, as if afraid somebody might overhear. "She is a minor."

"Right," I said flatly. "But she's also a mother now. Mothers do have rights about who can visit their child. I'm afraid we're following strict health and safety protocols on this ward, Mr - ?"

"Johnson."

"Mr Johnson – the baby is very premature, and at risk of infections. We therefore encourage the parents to limit visitors and, if they'd rather no visitors at all, then that's their prerogative."

"What are you saying? That she doesn't want to see us?"

"I'm saying that I shall need to ask her, Mr Johnson," I said. "And I shall return with her verdict. Please, wait here for me."

I turned away, leaving them blinking and embittered. I hoped I'd at least put them in their place a little. Lexie was a child, that was for sure, but she was also a mother – and it was our job to help empower her in that position, and encourage her to take over Tabby's care when it was time for her to go home. It wasn't for us to judge or guess at how such a situation came about – although with such un-supportive parents, I could hazard myself a guess – but it *was* our job to give the best care possible to both mother and baby.

I knocked on the door to nursery room two, knowing that Tabby was the only baby currently occupying it.

"Hello?" came Dr Hurst's voice.

"It's Max. Er, Dr Hartcliffe – I'd like to speak to Lexie, if I may," I said, keeping my mouth close to the frosted glass so she could hear me.

"Just a minute," said Dr Hurst. I heard the sounds of metal trays and equipment being scooped up and packed away. I waited what felt like ages. When the door opened, I barged my way in, wondering what the hell the hold-up was. Nina was tidying something away while Dr Hurst taped up a bandage around Lexie's arm.

"What's going on here?" I asked, going to Tabby's cot-side. She was dozing soundly. I picked up her chart and flipped through it, pleased to see that her levels had all remained within excellent margins.

Dr Hurst looked uneasy as she finished up with the bandage. Lexie avoided me with her head bowed, face hidden behind a curtain of greasy hair. I felt a light tap on my hand, and saw that it was Nina's hand gently knocking mine.

"What is it?" I whispered.

Nina turned her back to Lexie, busying herself with some packaging to deposit in the black bin behind us. She whispered so quietly that I almost missed it.

"Self-harm," said Nina in a hushed voice.

I breathed in deeply, realising this was an even worse situation than I thought. No wonder the poor girl was in the state she was in.

"Listen, Lexie. You've got some visitors. It's up to you if you want anybody coming in here to see you or the baby. If you don't want anybody, we'll simply disallow them and turn them away, all right?"

Lexie looked up from behind her curtain of hair with tears in her eyes. She didn't ask who it was – she clearly already knew.

"Tell them no," she said with a shaking voice. "I – I want to get used to my d-daughter without them here."

I nodded slowly, making eyes with Dr Hurst and Nina, who both looked relieved. "No problem at all," I said. "I'll let them know."

Before I had the chance to leave the room, the door burst open. It was Lexie's parents, barging their way in. Her father had a face as red as a fire truck.

"Woah, woah, woah – you can't just let yourself in here," I said, holding out my arms to usher them out again. "If you behave like that, I'll have to bring in security."

"Security? To see my own daughter? She's fourteen years old for Christ's sake!" The man spat the words so hard that I felt spittle raining on my skin.

"It's *you* we should be calling security about, trying to keep us away from our own child," said Lexie's mother, her face pinched and spiteful. The mother turned to Lexie, before looking over at the baby crib with an expression of disgust.

That look alone made me want to drag them out with my bare hands, but I couldn't – I'd be in too much trouble if I handled them physically, unless I had very good reason indeed.

"Just leave me alone, okay?" said Lexie, with pain in her voice. She didn't sound like an ordinary angsty teen – the way she sounded gave me real concern, especially with her bound-up wrist. How long had this child been in pain? Something told me it went far beyond the pregnancy. With parents like this, who were so visibly ashamed of her, I could understand why.

"Leave you alone? We gave you more space, Lexie, and look what happened. Look what you've done," said her father, bending over her with his hands on his hips.

"First all the weight problems, and now this. Well, at least I can understand where the weight gain came from this time," said Lexie's mother. "Are you insane, Lexie? Or you just like embarrassing us, is that it?"

I cleared my throat loudly, making them all turn to look at me. "I will not have raised voices around a baby, thank you," I said, trying to keep as clipped and diplomatic as possible. "And in any case, there are far too many people in this room to be in-keeping with our safety and hygiene policies."

That part was a bit of a fib, but sod them – if

they were going to treat their own daughter like that, then I would protect her. She was a mixed-up young lass with a newborn baby in the neonatal unit – she was suffering enough.

"If I want to reprimand my daughter I damn-well-will! You've embarrassed us for the final time, Lexie. And as for *that baby* – "

"Mr Johnson," Nina stepped forward, using a voice that even made me flinch. All heads turned to Nina. "Your daughter has been through far too much already. I understand that you'll both be in shock, but if you think I'm going to let you blow your top in my nursery in front of a 32 weeks gestation baby, you're mistaken."

The father looked at his wife with a cocky smirk that made me want to wipe it right off of him. He snorted, then, before breaking into a chuckle.

"Who's going to stop me? *You*? You stay out of this, nurse."

Nina put herself between Lexie and Mr Johnson as he made to storm up to his daughter. He laughed again, not taking her seriously. Nina was half his size, but she looked up at him with steely black eyes and an expression I'd never seen on her before: pure malice.

"If I have to tell you again, I will put out a call for security. You need to leave your daughter to rest and bond with her baby, Mr Johnson," said Nina through gritted teeth.

Now Mrs Johnson was leaping forward, shoving

her way in front of Nina. "You get the hell out of here right now. This is our daughter!"

"You were asked *not* to raise your voice," said Nina, but her warning was lost over the barrage of insults and complaints from both Mr and Mrs Johnson, who ranted and raved mindlessly without any thought to our patient or her mother at all.

Without warning, Mrs Johnson shoved Nina in the shoulders, making her stumble back.

"Mum! No!" Lexie cried.

Mr Johnson grabbed his wife at the elbows, hissing expletives in her ear as she lurched and lunged for Nina. Nina looked visibly shaken but remarkably calm.

I made eyes at Dr Hurst, who was way ahead of me – she hit the hidden security button behind the computer station to alert someone to come here, pronto. With Mr Johnson now yanking his wife around like a rag-doll, I decided I had no choice but to intervene. Blow whatever HR had to say about it.

In one movement I pulled Mr Johnson off of Mrs Johnson and held them both at arm's length, like two fighting alley cats. If Mr Johnson fancied himself a bit of a hard man, he was being given a no-nonsense reminder that he most certainly wasn't.

"Get your hands off me!" he snarled as I got him by the forearm.

"Dad?"

"Shut up, Lexie. I'm not done with you yet, not by a long shot!"

"This is all your fault," said Lexie's mother, struggling to free herself from my one-handed grasp.

"Nina, would you get the door for me please?"

"My pleasure, doctor," she said, opening the door leading into the hall.

I dragged the two disgraces along the hall like two tantruming toddlers. Nina followed me the whole way, opening doors for me until we made it out of the ward and into the hall, where two security officers were sprinting toward us.

"Escort these two off the hospital grounds, please, and ensure they don't come anywhere near this ward again," I said stiffly, handing them over. Mr Johnson spat in my direction, his saliva hitting me in the face.

"You're an overpaid *butcher*," said Mr Johnson. How many babies have you killed in surgery, eh? I bet it's hundreds."

I balled my fists, feeling rage boiling up inside me. Good god, I wanted to flatten the bastard. I wanted to paste him all over the floor. Nina stood firm beside me, radiating warmth. I could almost feel her telling me to remain calm, to keep my cool. To let this pass.

"Get him out of here before I call the police and report him for assault," I said through bared teeth. What I really *wanted* to say was very, very different.

As they took the Johnsons away, Nina and I made our slow way back to the ward, sharing a heavy silence between us.

"Do me a favour, Nina. I want you to make a very serious referral to social services – name me and Dr Hurst specifically – and see what support we can make available to Lexie and Tabby," I said.

"You read my mind," said Nina. "Couldn't agree more, doctor."

"There's no way we're letting them go back to a house with them in it. Not a chance. Be specific, won't you?"

"Of course," said Nina. "I won't be giving them any benefit of the doubt. Someone's got to look out for these children and it apparently isn't them."

I smiled warmly at her as my heart swelled. She'd been assaulted by Mrs Johnson and she barely batted an eyelid. "Don't leave out the part where you faced off two violent people," I said. "I'm proper impressed with you, Dorrington. I didn't know you had it in you."

She blushed and gave a sheepish smile. "Me either," she said. "I just wouldn't give a man like him the satisfaction of thinking he got to me."

I found myself reaching out to hold Nina's shoulder, giving it a firm pat. "Nice one, nurse," I said. "You did us proud today."

"Right back at you," she said. "Where are you off to now?"

"Me?" I sighed. "I'm going for a shower."

Nina raised her eyebrows as I walked away, just dreaming of the hot water now. As I entered the locker rooms and pulled off my scrub-top, I took out my phone and saw I had a single missed call and a voice note. It was from Hannah.

"Heey Dr Hard-on," she said in her sunny California accent. God, I so hated that she called me Doctor Hard-on. "Listen, babe, something serious has come up. I've got an actress with a pierced implant and it can't wait. I'm not going to be able to make my flight tonight. Another time, babe, okay? I'll talk to you later."

I frowned down at the phone before deleting the message with a sigh. Another cancellation. For an engaged couple, we barely ever saw each other – and I really meant *barely*. It had seemed like such a good idea at the time, when we were having near-constant sex and saw each other all day every day. But when she returned home to the USA, it was as if all that was forgotten. Damn, this wasn't like me – had I really been so dumb-struck by a beautiful American surgeon that I'd lost all sense of reason?

I felt guilty just for thinking it, but the feeling her cancellation had left me with was...relief. She didn't have time for us, and neither did I.

Maybe that was normal for a *power couple*, as she'd called us.

Or was it?

As I scrubbed myself clean in the shower, my

thoughts drifted to the beautiful woman who was dominating my thoughts, making my dick stir. I was appalled when I drifted out of my daydreaming to realise it wasn't Hannah that I was thinking about.

It was a little blonde nurse with fire in her eyes, protecting her patients, standing up against the people who threatened their peace. My insides twisted, and I felt light-headed to think of her. And to think that she'd become a mother, too, and had so much to navigate in her personal life as well as her job. I admired her. I admired Nina Dorrington more than I could express.

I found myself wondering, as I dried myself off with a towel, who the father was, and whether she was still seeing him. It was wrong to think of her that way; she was my colleague, and I was engaged. But an envy swirled around inside me as I thought of another man planting his seed in Nina, producing a child with her. It was a feeling I'd never, ever had before – not for any woman.

What the hell was going on with me?

# CHAPTER NINE
♥

*Nina*

Making the social services referral wasn't easy, but it was very much preferable to the alternative: leaving Lexie and Tabby to fight for themselves once they left the care of the hospital. We had one opportunity to do this right, and I was relieved that we were taking it.

The council would be sending somebody to visit Lexie over the weekend, and even though I wasn't scheduled to be in on Saturday, I promised I would be there. My only difficulty would be the inevitable: childcare.

"You can cover me, right, mum? It's only for an hour or two, tops. I have to be there for this girl – she's weak and she's in pain and she's got nobody else to look out for her. Nobody even knew the poor girl was pregnant," I said, stirring Maxina's porridge while I held my phone to my ear with my hunched shoulder.

"You've forgotten, haven't you?" said mum, making me stop in my tracks. Maxina raised her arms and screamed for her porridge. I put it down on her table and encouraged her into her chair, turning up the volume on the TV. If I could distract her for a few moments with cartoons, I might have a hope in hell of hearing this phone conversation.

"What? Forgotten what?" My heart pounded in my chest. There was no way I could let Lexie down; not in the state she was in. I couldn't let a young girl face a social services intervention alone with so much at stake – and besides, I'd promised her. I was a nurse. I kept my damn word.

Mum sighed on the other end of the line. "Darling, my cruise with Ted."

I tossed back my head and looked up at the ceiling in despair. There was a big splodge of dried red pasta sauce up there. How long had that been there? *Fuck, fuck, fuck.* Fuck Ted and fuck their fucking romantic cruise!

"We so seldom get away, darling, and you know I love to look after dear little Maxina, but I *have* given you plenty of notice. Ted's been held up with his foot operation, and you know his mobility hasn't been great – "

"Are you *certain* you can't reschedule it?"

Mum paused. "Well...not really, darling. It was booked over six months ago. It's a *cruise*, not a bus trip."

"Argh!" I groaned out-loud, realising I was doomed. Unless I could call around old friends – who I hadn't seen in over two years – to spirit up someone who could take care of my daughter, I was royally screwed. I would *have* to take Maxina into the hospital with me. I knew Max was scheduled in for the weekend, too – I would have a really tough time avoiding him, unless I got exceptionally lucky.

"It'll be all right, darling. All your colleagues will want to meet her, won't they?"

"*Yes*," I said, wiping my face with my free hand. Maxina tossed her spoon and flicked banana porridge across the TV screen. "But that's not the point. I really *can't* take Maxina into work."

"Why not?"

There was no way of explaining it to my mother. She would be beyond disappointed that I worked with the father, and worse, that I hadn't even informed the father of Maxina's existence. Well, she'd disappointed at first – and then unacceptably excited to discover Max Hartcliffe was Maxina's father. *At least he's a speciality surgeon*, she'd say. I couldn't bear the embarrassment of that – it would be worse than enduring her disappointment.

"Because...people ask too many questions, that's why. I'd rather just keep my family life private, you know?"

"But darling I know plenty of single working mothers. What on earth is there to be embarrassed about? You should be celebrating – my god, you're a *working mother*! When I had you and your sister it was all nappies and porridge and poo, and it all looked the same if I'm honest," said mum, chuckling.

I wiped a long smear of porridge from the TV with a wet-wipe and rolled my eyes. "Yeah, things have really changed since you were a parent."

"When your father died, I thought I'd never move on. When I met Ted, I thought I'd get all sorts of criticisms – I thought people would think that Ted was evidence that I'd never loved your father," said mum.

"Mum, please, let's not bring daddy into this – "

"But Nina, you've got to learn something here, darling. You've got to be brave and bold about who you are. Don't let the opinions of other people ruin a wonderful thing. You have a gorgeous little girl. Be proud of her. Show her off! For god's sake, you've earned it."

I listened, and I took mum's words to heart. I knew she was right.

But it still didn't solve my damn problem, because it wasn't one that anyone else could solve.

"So you're *definitely* not available for childcare on Saturday?" I asked, being facetious. But mum wasn't laughing, and the smile dropped from my face.

"No, darling. I think it's time you pulled up your big girl pants and faced these particular demons, or else they'll be chasing you forever."

Maxina looked up at me with her glittering sea-green eyes and smiled, chewing her plastic spoon.

I waggled my fingers down at her and let the swell of love go up and over me like a wave. Mum was right. I would have to bring Maxina to the hospital and take my chances on bumping into Max.

I just hoped none of my colleagues had a particular, niche penchant for recognising familial links via matching eye colours.

♥

I tugged Maxina's hat down, grateful that she had a full head of curly blonde hair to obscure her adorable but very-much-recognisable face. Marching the buggy across the car-park and into the main foyer, it felt weird to be in Sacred Heart when I wasn't on shift, especially out of uniform. I'd left that at home in the washing basket, but I did bring my identification lanyard so that the social worker knew I was a trusted person involved with Tabby and Lexie's care. Lexie's age and situation meant that it was reasonable to involve the help of social services – especially with Lexie's consent, which she'd gladly given.

The lift pinged open – empty, great – and I charged forward with the buggy, making Maxina giggle. No sooner had we begun our ascent did my rambunctious toddler decide that she'd very definitely had enough of her push-chair and wanted to be free.

"Typical," I said, as I unbuckled her. "I've gone and left your reigns at home."

Maxina pulled faces in the mirror against the

back end of the lift, totally oblivious to her mother's predicament. I sucked in a long, deep breath, dreading the sight of any large man with dark hair and a pale coat, knowing it could be Max. He would be lurking around the hospital somewhere, and I was crossing my fingers that we'd manage to slip by him unnoticed. We'd already had one of those mornings where everything went up in the air and it was a victory just to get us both in the car with our belts buckled, let alone make it here on time, and in one piece. The last thing I needed was to see Max and have to explain anything to him now.

"No worries, just focus," I said under my breath. "Just focus on the task ahead and everything will be all right."

"Chee-chee," said Maxina, groaning and lunging for the grey baby-changing rucksack I kept under the buggy.

"Now, now, Maxie, we're getting out of the lift soon," I said, gently guiding her hands away from the bag. Chee-chee – cheese puffs – were a must-have on any outing, and Maxina knew very-well that there'd be a bag of them waiting for her in the grey rucksack. But they were emergency cheese puffs, best used when mummy needed to do a lot of talking or concentrating, and I had planned to save them for Lexie's meeting.

"Chee-chee!"

"No, Maxie – come on, we're nearly there now."

Maxina balled up her fists, her bottom lip drawing up and wobbling. Oh lord, it was like watching a tsunami building – disaster was on the horizon if I didn't act quick.

"All right, all right – hang on a second," I said, hushing her while I rummaged in the rucksack. We were seconds from a tantrum and I couldn't find the sodding things. A vague memory drifted into my mind as my hands searched frantically – I saw myself clear as day, almost full-term with Maxina, declaring that I would be teaching discipline and self-control in myself and my baby, and that I would never, ever give in to demands just to placate a child on the brink of a tantrum.

Oh, how I laughed about that now.

"Ahah!" My hand landed on the bag of crisps just as the lift opened with a *ping*! "No, no, Maxina – come back here!"

Off she went at the sight of the doors opening, toddling as fast as her little legs could carry her – directly toward an open stairwell.

"No, Maxie!" I made to run after her but the buggy became wedged in the doors, blocking me. I shunted it to the right and cursed under my breath as it jammed. The break was still on! I stamped on it and shoved the buggy out, flustered and sweating. As I drew my eyes up from the buggy wheels, I first saw a pair of large feet in black slip-on shoes, then long muscular legs elegantly draped in blue surgical scrubs, followed by two strong, hairy arms that scooped Maxina up just as she reached the very top of a long staircase.

Oh god, if it wasn't him.

"Max," I said, catching my breath. "Thank you so much – she's an absolute menace. Maxie, you mustn't run from mummy like that!"

I froze as I realised I had said her name, and would have to explain it – but Max paid no attention at all, and I realised with great relief that he had his ear buds in, listening to music. Max bounced her on one arm, making her giggle and tip back her head. My terror at her face being revealed to Max was quickly replaced by one very keen observation – that Maxie seemed to *like* Max, instantly. Maxina was a shy baby who hated being held by anybody except me and my mother. Yet here she was, squealing with delight as Max bopped her.

"Well, look at you," said Max, removing an ear bud and slipping it into his scrub pocket. "She's just finding her freedom – aren't you?"

"Wow, she's taken to you right away," I said, my heart drumming so hard I was certain Max would hear it pumping through the tips of his stethoscope. I became all too aware of my sweaty, exhausted appearance; one that I took on whenever I had to run errands with child in-tow. It was impossible to look professional – or dare I say, pretty – when wrangling a toddler all day. At least, I never felt pretty.

"I've taken to her," said Max. "You know, she really looks like someone."

I clutched the handles of my buggy, ready to chuck Maxina in and make a dash for it if I had to. Max appeared to be in a very chirpy mood, but if he worked things out, he could turn in an instant, enraged, and I would have far too much explaining to do.

"Yeah?" I asked, my voice quavering.

Max turned his head to me with a cheeky grin that made my stomach do a flip. "You," he said, with a stubbly grin.

"Oh," I said breathlessly. "Yes, of course. My hair."

"It's a little curlier than yours though, isn't it?" He bopped Maxina again, smiling as she giggled. "Where's daddy today, huh?" Max glanced at me for the answer while the blood in my body froze to ice.

"W-what?" I asked, my voice faltering.

"Her daddy – couldn't he take her for you today?"

I frowned, searching Max's eyes for any hint of irony, and found none. He was being sincere.

"Uh, she, uh – her father is in Kampala. We uh – we agreed not to be in each other's lives. It's complicated. She doesn't have a dad. It's just, uh…it's just me and granny." I stumbled over my words so much that my mouth had gone dry, and I was left coughing into my sleeve.

"I see," said Max, swapping Maxina from one arm to another. "Well this little one has everything she needs, don't you, poppet? Motherhood looks good on you, Nina."

I blushed furiously, wishing I could just hide my face in my sleeve. Max paid no notice; he bopped Maxina until she threw her head back in another fit of giggles.

"I have to say, this is, uh, definitely a sight I didn't think I'd see any time soon," I said, holding my hand to the back of my neck.

"What do you mean?"

"I thought you – you know – *hated kids*," I said.

Max lowered Maxina and held her hand, guiding her toward the buggy. Bizarrely, she readily allowed him to strap her in with no fuss.

"They're annoying, they're demanding, they're messy – but I love kids really," said Max. "I just couldn't see myself with one, you know? Certainly not at the start of my career, when I had so little time. I barely have any now. It's just something I guess I missed the boat on."

"I see," I said, feeling as though I might faint right there on the spot. Looking at his handsome face and glittering, soft, kind eyes behind a façade of power and the potential for brutality riddled me with guilt and shame. It enveloped me in a dark choke-hold. I realised in that moment just how wrong I had been, and I knew I had to tell him.

This had gone on long enough.

"M-Max – "

"Hey, it's 11.00 a.m. – weren't you meeting Lexie and the social worker now?" he asked, checking his phone for the time. "You'd better get going. Did you bring your lanyard? I can buzz you through if you need me to."

"Oh god, how can that be the time? I'm sorry, Max, I have to dash – thanks for helping with the baby!" I called out to him as I ran, shoving the buggy ahead of me.

"Don't mention it," he said, his voice falling away behind me.

♥

Lexie, when I arrived in the play-room, was holding Tabitha carefully in her bandaged arms. It was a very promising sign. Tabby's incubator was by her side – another great sign if Dr Hurst had deemed Tabby to be fit enough to be moved around the ward.

"I'm so sorry I'm running a little late," I said, making Lexie look up from the baby she cradled in her arms. "Though I think I got away with it. I take it she isn't here yet?"

"Who?" asked Lexie.

I unbuckled Maxina and let her roam among the dolls house, the rocking horse, and the musical baby-walker, clutching her bag of cheese puffs.

"The social worker?"

"Oh, yeah – she's not here yet," said Lexie,

sounding as if she'd been completely lost in her own thoughts. She turned and looked back at her baby, wrapped up nicely in a baby blue knitted blanket – one of the knitting donations from our premature babies campaign.

For a moment I was worried, but then I studied Lexie's face and realised that she wasn't being distant – she was transfixed by her baby. She was falling in love. We sat for a moment in silence, and I let Lexie drink in the pure joy of holding her own child in her arms. *This* was the bonding time she needed, away from any drama or judgement or toxicity at home.

Within moments the social worker arrived; a brunette with dark eyes like mine, dressed in a casual suit and flat shoes.

"Lexie? It's nice to meet you and Tabitha – my name's Clara Murphy. I'm with the children and families social work team."

"Hello," said Lexie in a weak voice, hiding behind her curtain of hair. I noticed how she held Tabby closer to her, as if afraid she might be snatched right out of her arms.

"And you're – ?"

"I'm the staff neonatal nurse you spoke to on the phone – Nina Dorrington," I said, holding out my hand for her to shake. "That's my daughter playing over there."

"It's lovely to meet you," said Clara. She shrugged off her suit jacket and slung it over the back of her armchair, before crossing one leg over another and sitting back. Anybody would think we were just meeting for coffee.

"All right. If we're all comfortable, shall we start at the beginning?"

At first Lexie gave very short, meek answers that could barely be heard over Maxina's babbling in the background. With gentle coaxing and casual conversation between myself and Clara, with me filling in the odd detail about Tabby's care, Lexie visibly began to relax. Soon she was giving more details about her birth at school, and she gave hints here and there of the atmosphere at home. One thing that was becoming very clear was that Lexie's home would not be a good environment for her and the baby, and she had no confidence that her parents would be a support – a sentiment I agreed with after their aggression on the ward.

"What would a good home environment for yourself and Tabby look like to you?"

Lexie bowed her head. I noticed a tear fall, so I passed her a box of tissues we kept on the coffee table. She took one and dabbed her face, still rocking little Tabby in her arm.

"Where I can look after her and still do my school work," she said very softly. The end of her sentence had an upwards inflection, as if she wasn't at all sure whether she was even entitled to have both.

"It may be that we have to think outside the box

a little, because of your age – but it could be that we discuss moving you to a mother and baby unit, where you can have space to adjust whilst also being supervised yourself. It is a little tricky, but I think we can figure something out," said Clara. "Is there anybody else – an adult in your family, for example, who could help and support you?"

Lexie shrugged. "My nan, but she lives an hour away and I don't see her much. I do love my nan."

"What about Tabby's father and his family?" Clara asked gently.

Here, Lexie clammed up and didn't speak for a few moments. Eventually she said, in a very small voice, "He doesn't know. I mean, he knows I had a baby...everybody knows. But he won't know she belongs to him."

"Who is he?" Clara pressed gently.

"A boy in my class," said Lexie.

Her answer seemed genuine – Clara and I shared a brief glance. No doubt she was feeling as relieved as I was that it wasn't someone inappropriate, and that we didn't have to get the police involved. Things were complicated enough for Lexie without throwing that into the mix too.

"Maybe we can start a dialogue with him and his family, if that's something you're open to?" asked Clara.

Lexie shook her head slowly. "He pretends I don't exist."

"What do you mean?" I asked, wondering how a

baby could have been made if the boy in question didn't even acknowledge Lexie.

"I mean – we were...we were boyfriend and girlfriend, sort of. But it was all a secret. He – he said he loved me, but he was too ashamed to admit it to his friends. They all think I'm a freak."

"You are most certainly not a freak," I said, reaching out and patting Lexie's shoulder. I was glad that these details were coming out now in front of Clara, who could help her access mental health support as well as finding a way for her to take care of Tabitha *and* keep her own identity as a growing teen.

"I think the first step will be for you and me to have a chat about how we can start communicating with all the right people. Tabby's here now, everyone knows – so why hide her?"

Lexie nodded, rocking her gently in her arms. It was evident to me that her love for Tabby was growing rapidly, and soon she would find the courage to face the world with her daughter, just like I had.

Except Lexie was agreeing to communicate with the father of her child, and that was a damn sight more than I had managed. Max didn't even *know* he was a father.

I realised in that moment, as I watched Maxina play, that a traumatised teen had more courage than I did, and I was a grown woman in my thirties. That had to change. I had to tell him.

My excuses had officially run out.

# CHAPTER TEN
♥

*Max*

I tossed and rolled in bed, fighting demons in my sleep. It had been a long while since I'd had a nightmare like this one.

Fire blazed before me, four storeys high. The crying of a baby – no, perhaps a little older – came wailing from a window high up in the attic of a burning house. The scene developed before me as my eyes adjusted and took it all in, details spawning as I moved my head, loading up like a video-game. The baby's wailing continued, and the inferno raged. Adrenaline pumped through me like a crash-call and I ran for the front door, smashing against it with my shoulder.

The door gave way, breaking off into splinters as if rotted through. It opened onto a hall with a staircase, from which came billowing plumes of smoke. I could somehow breathe despite the acrid cloud, and without thinking I barrelled through it, taking the stairs two and three at a time. Up, and up, I went; but the baby's wailing seemed to only get farther away. As I reached the very top of the house, panting, my eyes streaming, I threw myself against the remaining door where the crying sound rang out clear as the siren of a blue-lighted ambulance. This time I made no impact, with the door staying firm – and only when I fell in a heap before it, did the door creak slowly open.

As I opened my eyes, the black smoke – the whole inferno – had disappeared. There was only a large empty room with a cot waiting by the window, and a little girl sitting inside. She could only be a year or so old, with curly blonde hair and a hat pulled down over her eyes. As I heaved myself up and approached her, I felt as though I were wading through invisible mud – lifting each limb very slowly, the mud pulling me and preventing me more with every movement.

When I eventually reached the cot-side, blood was thumping between my ears. The little girl babbled, playing with a small stuffed rabbit with a bandaged paw. My hand reached out of its own accord in slow motion, my fingers clutching the top of the baby's hat. As I drew the hat away, the baby looked up at me with a beautiful, sunny smile. Her sea green-blue eyes glittered up at me, eyes that I knew. My eyes.

I sat bolt-upright in bed, panting, my back sweating. I hadn't had one of those shitty slow-motion dreams in a long, long time, not since I was a fledgling surgeon taking on my first cases. I used to dream that I was trying to access a patient in cardiac arrest, or trying to get back to my place at the operating table, and the invisible mud would be stopping me.

It meant that I had a big-bastard problem; something I was avoiding. Yeah, no shit, Sherlock. As I blinked rapidly in the darkness, letting my eyes adjust, I tried to recall the child in my dream; the one who seemed so eerily familiar. Was it Nina's child I'd seen? Wearing the hat she wore that day in the hospital? My stomach lurched and I groaned out loud, hoping I got to the bathroom in time. I flew from the bed and got my head over the basin just in time for the contents of my stomach to rush from my throat and hit the back of the pan.

I was working too much; I was always working too much. What else was I supposed to do? Keep checking my phone like a love-sick school-boy, hoping to have a text from Hannah? She hadn't responded to me in days. Even her secretary sounded pitying on the phone, explaining that she'd been carried away by this or that, or had another surgery that simply couldn't wait, and that she'd catch up with me at the weekend. Except, of course, she never did catch up with me.

I popped open the medicine cabinet and took out my toothbrush, toothpaste, and floss. I examined my rugged face in the mirror; my stubble with its flecks of grey, the wrinkles at the corners of my eyes, all the signs of ageing that reminded me I wasn't young anymore. Surgery was my life; my heart and soul. I could never take that from another person – certainly not somebody I respected as much as I respected Hannah. I understood, after all, that she was obsessed with her own work. But what sort of relationship was this, really?

*The best you're going to get at your age*, I told myself. It was delusional to think I could date another surgeon and actually expect to see one another.

As I buzzed away with my electric toothbrush and watched my mouth froth up like a rabid dog, I wondered who on earth would want a big lump like me sharing a bathroom with them? Perhaps it really did make sense to have a long-distance marriage, where we focused on our careers. What could a man my age expect?

I should be grateful for Hannah. Right?

As I got showered and dressed, wolfing down a cup of tea and a slice of dry toast, the sick feeling never left me. It gnawed away at my insides like a virus, only I didn't feel otherwise unwell. What was going on with me? I tried to recall my dream as I shrugged on my jacket and lanyard over my shirt and jumper, but it was no use. The images had faded, only leaving me with the sickening feeling that something just wasn't right.

Leaving the room, I bumped straight into Dr Hurst, still holding her car-keys. She raised an eyebrow.

"You're not still living in the doctors' mess? Jesus Christ. You're due to be married!"

"I know, I know – don't lay it on thick," I said gruffly, walking with her toward the main building.

Since my break-up with Rebecca, I'd been living in all kinds of temporary accommodations, until my work piled up so much that it made more sense to live in the surgeons' mess on-site. When you performed as many surgeries as I did, nobody batted an eyelid about where I stayed – it made more sense to never leave. Before I knew it, years had gone by, and I no longer felt comfortable with the idea of getting a place all to myself. I'd been adrift ever since, keeping quiet about my living arrangements to avoid any pitying looks. It made me look like a loner – and all right, in some respects I was one – but I was also a trusted physician. Nobody trusted a loner. Protecting my image to patients and peers was important.

And here Dr Hurst was, taking the piss.

"Seriously, Max. I feel like I'm the friend trying to encourage you to move out of your parents' basement," said Dr Hurst.

"Leave it out, smart-arse," I said. "It's called being frugal. I've a lot to save up for."

"It's called being tight. What's a man on your salary need to do to get himself a decent apartment in London?"

"Why do you care?" I asked, snapping. "Scrub that last. I'm a grumpy bugger in the morning."

"It's not morning, Max – we're on a late shift, remember?"

"Fuck," I said, shaking my head. I ran my fingers through my hair. "I'm literally losing the plot, here."

"You need to take a break, Max, seriously. Have a holiday. Or are you holding out for the honeymoon?" Dr Hurst led the way to the break room, where we could grab a coffee before the next handover. Dr Bellamy was already inside, pouring himself a cup.

"Evening, Max," he said, taking a sip.

"Thought it was morning," I said, pinching the bridge of my nose. "Jesus, I need to be sleeping better than this. I feel like I'm on a rotten hangover."

"Well, are you?" asked Dr Bellamy.

I scowled at him. "No."

"He's having second thoughts about the wedding," said Dr Hurst, winking at me. For some reason she irritated me, even though I knew she was playing. I felt my hackles rising and I had to resist the urge to bite her head off.

"I'm having second thoughts about bringing you on as my protegé," I told her. "If you've any hope of scrubbing in today, you'd best keep comments like that to yourself."

"Jesus," said Dr Hurst, rolling her eyes. "Doctor grumpy today."

"I'm serious," I said. "I'm in no mood."

"All right, all right," said Dr Hurst. "Let's talk shop, then. There's a patient in nursery room one I need you to take a look at. Ari, 30 weeks. He's stable on the whole, but I've observed some bloating. He's been relying a little more on his oxygen feed the last couple of days, too. I just wanted your opinion."

"No problem," I said. "How does he present?"

"Mostly, fine. He's been doing great. We've had a slight spike in temperature, but it corrected itself each time. Just every now and then we're getting a few digestive issues, potentially – with the distended abdomen, I mean."

"Stools?"

"Wet, loose. No blood or mucus."

"Have you run bloods?"

"All came back within normal regions."

I poured myself a small cup of warm coffee and chugged it down.

"We'll do an ultrasound and have a look at his gut. If it's a bowel issue we'll need to know about it pronto so I can book him into the OR," I said.

♥

As I guided the ultrasound probe over Ari's tiny abdomen, I noticed a little distension – nothing too serious for now. Apart from some potential inflammation, I couldn't see anything wrong.

"We'll keep observing him today. Something's up, but it's not obvious yet quite what it is," I told Dr Hurst. "I'm not overly concerned."

"No problem," she said. "Oh, Max? You might want to catch up with Nina – she's on shift tonight. Sounds like she made some real progress with Tabby's mum."

"Right-o," I said, slotting Ari's notes back inside his cot-side and making my way out toward the nurse's station.

Nina was there, inputting something into the computer. When she saw me she paled, her eyes widening.

"You don't have to look like you've seen a bloody ghost," I said, wondering what the hell her problem could be now. One moment she seemed relaxed around me, and the next it was as if she was afraid of me. She was setting me on edge, making me uncomfortable in my own sodding environment. No wonder I couldn't keep my head on straight lately; I didn't belong anywhere.

Not here, not in the doctors' accommodations, where I couldn't even get a decent wink of sleep. Maybe Dr Hurst was right. Maybe I did need a vacation. Maybe it was time I moved on for good, and that my wedding to Hannah couldn't come soon enough.

Not that we'd spent enough time together since she flew back to even begin the arrangements. It was all beginning to feel like a pipe dream, now; like everything was loose and up in the air. Wasn't it always, when it came to me?

"I'm sorry, I was – I was miles away," said Nina, stuttering.

"You had the meeting with Lexie and the social worker?"

Nina's shoulders relaxed, then – she looked relieved to have been given something to talk about.

"Yes! They're looking into some temporary accommodation for her, outside of the family home, but with proper supervision. Her parents have been sadly – although maybe surprisingly – non-compliant. It's a mother and baby unit for teen mums who need trusted adults around for support," said Nina. "Lexie's really keen to give it a try."

"Good, good. And the father?"

"A boy in her class," said Nina, giving me a relieved smile.

"Good stuff," I said. "You did some great work there, Nina. I appreciate it."

I made to move away onto the next task before I did my rounds, but Nina tapped my arm and made me whip around to face her. She flinched at my sudden movement, like a mouse.

"Erm...I wanted to ask you, er..."

I frowned, watching her search for the right

words. "I'm pressed for time, here," I said.

"H-h-how's you and your fiancé doing?"

I folded my arms, wondering what the hell Hannah had to do with anything. "She's fine," I said, prepared to leave it at that. But Nina's expectant face triggered something in me, and I found myself wanting to vent.

"Being a bit avoidant, if you must know. This whole long-distance thing isn't turning out quite as well as I hoped." I felt a small amount of weight lifting from my shoulders. Why had it taken Nina to ask the question for me to feel able to answer it?

"They say absence makes the heart grow fonder," said Nina, with a hopeful look in her eye that I didn't quite understand.

"Whoever came up with that bollocks needs their head examining," I said, unable to hide my bitterness. "Absence just creates more absence, if you ask me."

Nina's eyes welled with what looked like tears, but it could have been a trick of the lights. She had a long night ahead of her – maybe she'd used a few eye drops.

"Y-you don't think that maybe being away from somebody might make you – I don't know – want them even more?"

I frowned, wondering why Nina was so invested in my long-distance relationship.

"No, I don't. I think it leads to frustration."

Well, at least I'd managed to hit the nail on the head. *Frustrated* was definitely the right word. I was pent-up and feeling bloody-well abandoned, and I couldn't explain that to anyone. I couldn't even tell Hannah because she was always unavailable, and she was supposed to be my poxy fiancé.

Nina's eyes seemed to be searching mine, and I wondered if those were tears after all. But why would they be? Why would Nina have tears for me?

"Do you –" she stopped herself.

"Spit it out," I said, getting increasingly impatient.

"Do you love her, Max?"

I blinked, unfolding my arms. I straightened my back. "You what?" I asked.

Nina lowered her voice, glancing to one side as another nurse brushed by.

"You just don't seem...you don't seem like a man in love, that's all."

Who the hell was she to make an observation like that, right out of the blue? I wrinkled my nose in disgust, snatching up the print-out of the evening's patients that had been left on the desk, ready for the evening handover.

"What sort of question is that to ask me, nurse?" Even as I snapped at her, I wished I could take the words back. I wished I could stuff them back into my big fat gob, but instead I kept on going. "You mind your own business, Nina, do you understand?"

She shrunk inside herself, recoiling from me. I realised Dr Bellamy, the admin staff, and a bundle of nurses and healthcare assistants were glancing uneasily our way, hearing the awful tone in my voice. I wanted to take it back, but I couldn't, and I looked like a prize arsehole for it.

"Handover," I bellowed. "Huddle up, people."

♥

Around 3.00 a.m., I found myself pacing the hall outside the ward like a restless bear. My agitation had only increased as the shift went on, and I found myself realising some ugly, awful truth that I had apparently been running from.

I was not in love with Hannah, and she was not in love with me.

"Who the fuck am I kidding?" I asked under my breath, running my hand over my stubble in frustration. This was no way to begin a relationship, let alone a marriage. I whipped out my phone and dialled Hannah's number. Then I hung up, and did a video call instead. She was my poxy fiancé – the least she could do was answer my calls and actually look at my face.

To my surprise, she actually answered. Her angelic face and surgery-precision nose came into view, framed by long locks of white-blonde hair. Her lips were plumped up with filler – that was a new one on me. She hadn't done anything to her lips when I'd last seen her – god, was it really so many months ago now?

"Babe, I'm totally swamped – what is it?"

I frowned. "Nice way to greet your husband-to-be."

She sighed, shaking her head. "I'm so sorry, Max. It's my fault. I'm just so tired, and so swamped all the time. With the time difference...it's just been so hard getting back to you. I really wanted to, though."

"Did you?"

She paused. "Of course. What's up with you?"

I paused a moment as a staff member walked by, buzzing themselves into the ward with their lanyard.

"Look, Hannah – this is difficult, but I think it needs to be said. It's been driving me crazy. You and me – we had our good times, but...this isn't love, is it?"

She bowed her head, her white-blonde hair falling in front of her face. When she looked up, she had a look of resignation that I felt in my core. She knew it too.

"Maybe we...I don't know. Maybe we jumped the gun."

We shared a silence.

"I think maybe we did," I said softly.

"I don't know what to say," said Hannah, her voice breaking up half-way through. This was what our lives together were, at best: a flaky signal and a complete loss of connection.

"I think we've said it all," I said. "No hard feelings, all right?"

"I meant what I said at the time, Max...but you're right. I guess...I guess this isn't love, after all," she said. "No hard feelings."

"I'll – I'll see you around, Hannah," I said, before ending the call.

And with it, ended my hopes and dreams of working in the city of angels, living the high life in Beverley Hills. A Yorkshire boy in an LA. Who'd have thought it. I pocketed my phone, wiping a hand over my face. I really did need a holiday.

Dr Hurst came running into the hall. "Nursery room one," she said, looking flustered. "I want you to take a look at this."

I ran after her, sparing no more thought to the fact that my engagement had just ended. When we arrived in nursery room one, Nina was frantically jotting down numbers on Ari's chart – and when I looked around, I realised why. There was a significant vomit, and Ari's belly looked distended beyond belief – as if it had been literally inflated with air. The baby boy began to cry, his face screwing up and turning a deep red.

I felt his abdomen with two fingers, detecting a swollen and lumpy bowel. As Nina followed Dr Hurst's instructions and hooked Ari up to saline, I watched her; saw her determination, her concern for the baby, her dedication to the role, to the hospital. To us, her team.

To me.

Sometimes the answers were so obvious, that they were staring you right in the bloody face; but if you weren't willing to look, or didn't have the damn guts to really see…then you could stay blind to them.

"Lactose intolerance, Dr Hurst," I said. "The baby's allergic to the milk feeds."

"Of course," she said, shaking her head. "I'm sorry, Max. I should have seen it was something as simple as that."

"We can't be sure of it just yet, but run the appropriate tests and get him off the lactose. I've got a very good hunch that I'm right," I said.

I gently held Nina by the elbow, giving her a light tug as I left the room. She flinched again, but this time I wasn't flooded with anger. For the first time in a long while, I let my guard down and relented to the feelings that had been hiding under my layers and layers of frustration.

"Nina – break room, now. I want a word."

# CHAPTER ELEVEN

♥

*Nina*

My stomach churned as I followed Max to the break room, keeping my head bowed. I knew he was on the rampage lately, but to be barked at and humiliated several times in one shift – well, it was enough to make me want to transfer to another hospital. I'd tried to get through to him; to gauge whether he could have feelings for Maxina even though he'd never known her, and all I'd managed to do was irritate him. Now, apparently, I'd really pissed him off.

But how was I ever going to broach the subject when he was so quick to bite my damn head off?

To my surprise, when we reached the break room, Max carried on through to the bunk room, where we kept the beds. Now I knew I was really in for it. If he wanted that much privacy, then he was really going to lay into me.

"Close the door," he said bluntly. My hands

shook as I pushed it shut, leaning against it to keep as far from Max as possible.

"What you said earlier –" Max began, his eyes aflame with anger.

"It was inappropriate. It was wrong. I'm sorry – "

"Shut up a minute so I can think," he said, pacing back and forth between the bunk beds. I shook my head in disbelief, wishing I could give him a piece of my mind. I could, but saying something I might regret meant putting my job at risk – and then what would happen to me and Maxina?

"You were right about Hannah," he said, stopping in his tracks and turning to face me. "I ended it with her this evening."

"Oh god, Max. I'm so sorry. If I – if I interfered, I really didn't mean to. I just – "

Why *had* I interfered? Why had I said anything about it *at all*?

"No, no – Nina, it's all right. You've – you've helped me to think more clearly. I can see now what it is that's been bothering me."

*Oh god*, I thought. He was realising he was Maxina's father, and now I would have to tell him straight.

"Max..."

He closed his eyes and swallowed hard. He looked exhausted and somehow tense, all at once – like a balled up mess of fury that was fast running out of the energy required to sustain itself. Like he needed some kind of release.

"I tried to tell you. I...tried to explain. I – "

Max paced slowly towards me, and was looking down at me now with eyes that could burn two holes right through me. He seemed furious and yet reluctant, paralysed with indecision about just what to do. Was he about to fire me?

"I – "

"Shut up, Nina," he said softly, making me glance up in confusion. He was standing so close, his body was almost pressing against mine. "Just stop talking."

Max grabbed me by the waist and pulled me against his hard, warm body. I cried out, startled, but he held a finger to my lips and silenced me. As he drew his finger away, he let his hand cup the back of my head and draw my face to him, parting my lips with his and kissing me long, slow, and deep. I realised then that he was rigid, his hard length bulging from inside his pants.

Without thinking a moment longer, I found myself giving in to a ball of energy that had been spinning inside *me*, wanting to explode. I threw my arms around Max's neck and jumped into his arms, letting him catch me under my thighs as my legs encircled his waist. His tongue dove greedily into my mouth as he backed up towards the waiting beds, his large hands cupping my buttocks and squeezing them. He turned and threw me down, shrugging off his coat. He lifted his shirt and jumper off over his head and tossed them away in one move, giving me a view of his hard muscles, broad shoulders, and the perfect T-shape of his upper body.

I lay back on my elbows, my clit throbbing at the sight of him looming over me; breathing hard as he unbuckled his belt. I popped open my tunic and threw off my bra, my eyes lingering on his pants as he tugged them down. He released his huge, thick member; as juicy and hard as I remembered.

"Let me," he said, pulling off my lace panties. "I want to savour this."

I laid back and sighed deeply, arching so that my breasts and their hard nubs protruded invitingly. My vaginal walls pulsed with longing. God, how I'd wanted this. For years, I'd wanted this.

Max kissed my inner thigh once, twice, making his way down between my legs. When he kissed my labia I sighed, my nipples aching and throbbing as his touch sent sensations rippling through me. He made love to me with his lips and tongue, his mouth encircling my clit and tugging, pulling, until my legs were wide open as I ground against his face.

I was gasping and thrusting when he lifted my bottom half up and positioned himself between my legs, his cock fully erect and bobbing upright.

"Have you wanted this, Nina, like I have?" he asked, his voice thickened and ragged with lust. "Even now, I stroke my cock and I think of you."

I groaned, opening my legs wider and drawing my ankles in. He held my knees, massaging them, as he looked down at me with half-lidded eyes.

"Do you want me, darling?" he asked.

I panted, wanting him so badly that my womb ached. "I think of you when I come," I said, gasping. "I lay in the bath and I masturbate, thinking of you."

It was appalling, speaking like this in our place of work – a place where, moments ago, I had been the absolute professional.

And that's why I wanted him so badly. That's why it felt so good.

Max stroked his cock and let his hand drift down to my clitoris, toying it expertly with his thumb. My eyes fluttered closed and I let my head fall back on the pillow, mewling softly as he brought me close to climax.

"My beautiful Nina," he said softly. His hand moved from his cock to tweak my nipples, sending electric waves throughout my body. "I need to be inside you."

"Yes." I panted, my vagina aching to be filled. "Yes, Max, yes."

Max lifted me under my knees and prodded my opening with the rounded, swollen head of his cock. He prized me open and slid inside, groaning aloud as he reached the neck of my womb. I held up my thighs and made room for him, feeling stuffed full and ready to grind myself to ecstasy.

But Max had other plans. His thumb found my clit and he swirled it, pressing and releasing, until my pussy throbbed and ached to release. At the point when I could take no more and began bucking, Max fucked me hard, going at me like a piston, until he was crying out my name.

On the sound of his release I came hard, the orgasm rocking my whole body in luscious waves of pure pleasure. His thumb pressed hard and tight, ensuring it lasted as long as possible. I cried into my pillow, stuffing my face with it, while Max's cock pulsed and spurted his thick, hot juices deep inside me.

He grunted like an animal when he finished, sliding out of me and curling me up in his arms. Our naked bodies were warm, fitting together like a plug in a socket. He kissed me long and slow, and I melted into the safety of his embrace.

He gently drew his lips away and cupped my face in one hand, inviting me to meet my gaze with his.

"What's her name?" he asked, his voice so soft I could have missed it. "You never told me her name."

I froze momentarily, shaking. He hadn't been fooled at all. A part of me urged me to keep silent, to say nothing, to say in this safe cocoon I had created. But I wasn't playing games anymore, and neither was he. Clearly.

"Maxina," I said.

He held his forehead to mine, smiling gently. Was he really, truly, smiling?

"Why didn't you tell me she was mine?"

I couldn't answer him. Wasn't the answer obvious? Couldn't he infer it for himself?

"Because I was afraid." It was all I could say, but at least it was honest.

Max paused, kissing my forehead. I tensed up, not knowing where this would go now, or what it would lead to. My deep seated fear was returning.

"You named her after me and you?"

I nodded, breathing fast. Max caught me by surprise, sending a bolt of electricity through me, straight to my clitoris, as he gently pinched my nipple between his thumb and forefinger. I moaned out-loud, my hand reaching out to claw the bed-sheet. I felt his warm seed oozing out of me.

His lips found mine before travelling in kisses down to my breast, where he pulled and suckled my nipple, making me roll my hips and groan.

"Why didn't you tell me, Nina?" he asked breathlessly against my nipple, before he resumed toying me with his tongue.

He guided me over onto my belly with one turn of his hand at my waist, and I found myself face-down, holding onto the pillow. Max slid his new erection deep inside me, making me gasp as he took me right to the hilt. He cupped me under my breasts and massaged them as he fucked me, long and slow, building up to a crescendo within moments. Soon he was bucking hard and pounding me, filling me with his seed once more.

My clit rubbed against the bed-sheet, and with his cock stuffing my vagina full, I found myself helpless to another wave of intense orgasm, even harder than the first. I cried out into the pillow, my muscles tensing as I reached my peak and exploded into a thousand pieces.

Max, breathing hard, slid out of me and flopped down beside me. He rested his head on one arm and let the other curl around me. I snuggled into his embrace, my vaginal walls pulsing with the absence of him.

"You should have told me, Nina," he said firmly. "But I...I think I understand why you felt you couldn't."

"You do?" I asked, glancing up at him. Could he be serious?

"I'm not an easy man to approach. I know that," he said. "But I...we..." He seemed to lose his words, but I sensed the thread of where he was going.

"We need to figure this out," I said. "If...if that's what you want, too."

He pulled me close and kissed the crown of my head.

"When can I see my daughter?" he asked softly. I thought I detected something I was sure I would never, ever hear in the voice of Max Hartcliffe.

Fear.

"As soon as you like," I said, my arm encircling his waist. "If you want to, you can come with me to collect her from my mother."

He tensed a little, wiping his brow with a swipe of his hand.

"What if she doesn't like me?" he asked.

"Of course she'll like you. She'll love you. She loved you the minute you picked her up," I said, glancing up at him incredulously.

"Not Maxina," he said. "I mean your mother."

♥

If only I hadn't been so swept up in my desire for Max, I would have remembered something pretty crucial.

In all the time since I'd given birth to Maxina, I'd had no intention at all of sleeping with anybody else. How could I, with a baby to take care of? And besides, there was nobody else I desired – certainly not since *him*.

And so, quite reasonably –

I hadn't started up any new birth control.

# CHAPTER TWELVE

♥

*Max*

I sat up in bed, watching the rain fall hard against the window pane; it was a sound that should be lulling me to sleep, but it wasn't. Besides, I never slept properly when I was on-call, knowing I would need to spring into action at any moment. I could still smell Nina on me; the soft scent of her soap and remnants of her floral perfume. Sometimes I could taste her, even after taking another shower. My head was swimming with unanswered questions, giving me palpitations. I drew up my knees and leaned over them, watching the rain.

There were so many things I didn't know, that I should know. I was a father, for fuck's sake. A father to a child I didn't realise I had for well over a year.

Did Maxina sleep well in the rain, or did she wake up, scared, needing a hug? Was she healthy?

Did she want for anything? I thought of all those nursery fees and felt sick to my stomach, knowing I should have paid them all. I should have been there for her – and Nina, too. To think that she'd gone into labour in a foreign country, all alone, while I was...what would I have been doing? Surgery? Sleeping with Hannah, as if I hadn't a care in the world?

I leapt off the bed and paced the room. The moonlight flooded in through the window to cast my shadow on the floor.

Hannah. How would I explain all this to Hannah, if I ever saw her again? She was supposed to have been my fiancé, and all the while I was a father to a little girl with a member of my own staff. It was all kinds of messed up, and yet I didn't feel furious; I merely felt...insecure. Doubtful. Unsafe.

I didn't know the first thing about looking after children. They were biology to me; puzzles to solve. Once I solved them, they could become human again and go back to their mums and dads. They weren't *mine* to love.

"Fine thing for a neonatal surgeon to say for himself," I said out-loud, chuckling. There was nothing remotely funny about it – but regardless, it was the truth.

Then there was Nina. I'd already let her down by backing out of her offer to pick up Maxina and meet her mother. After I'd sated my lust, my mind had cleared, making way for all my fear and anxiety, and it had all gotten too much. I needed time away to think and get my head around this. Nina had understood – of course she had, ever the caring nurse that she was – but it didn't help. I still wasn't able to make head nor tail of the fact that I, Max Hartcliffe, had a child.

She was walking around, breathing the same air as me, looking up at the same sky with my eyes.

*Why, Nina? Why didn't you trust me enough to tell me?*

Fury filled me, but it soon turned to shame, as if somebody had poured a big bucket of cold water over that feeling. I just couldn't blame Nina – she must have been scared herself, but of me? Really?

I went to the bathroom, turned on the light and looked at my reflection in the medicine cabinet. How could Nina want me to take her to bed, but also be afraid of me? Granted, we knew each other better now – a lot better now – than we did when Maxina was conceived. Back then, our attraction and love-making was purely a sexual thing – a matter of convenience. I'd woken with a stiffy and there, beside me, was a gorgeous little blonde with a hot body, and she wanted me too. What hot-blooded male could resist Nina Dorrington when she looked up at him with lust in her eyes, her legs begging to be parted?

I leaned against the sink unit and let out a long, uneasy breath. Here came the guilt again, cloaking me in shame like a big wet blanket. My cock stiffened just at the thought of Nina, and it was clouding all sense of judgement. I couldn't come to terms with fatherhood while fantasizing about Nina – our coupling could be confusing for Maxina if there wasn't really a relationship there. The fact was that we had never yet had the chance to explore one. We'd never even dated.

And nor should we, given that until last night, I had been engaged to another woman. Hannah was a highly respected plastic surgeon among Hollywood royalty, and a good woman – even if she wasn't the love of my life after all. She deserved more respect than this.

And so did my daughter.

I needed to know exactly where we stood with one another; to understand how we were going to go about making this work, and what that actually constituted. When I thought of Nina, I felt a mixture of lust, anger, and...what was that? Nausea?

Could it be that Nina and all that she represented actually scared me?

My pager bleeped wildly from its place beside the bed, jolting me from my muddled thoughts. Thank goodness for my career, I thought – who needed these thoughts when I could rely on action to see me through?

I splashed my face with cold water and ran to the bedroom, flicking on the light. I pulled on fresh briefs, a white T-shirt and a pair of clean, pressed trousers from the wardrobe, my heart racing, knowing I didn't have another minute to spare.

♥

"Hurst, Bellamy – scrub in, it's your lucky day. You're going to want to see this!" I bellowed.

An emergency call-out had come from the A&E department of a hospital two hundred miles away; they were transferring a labouring woman to us via air ambulance, and we'd be rushing her directly into the OR for caesarean section and an immediate operation on her newborn child. A quick scan had told the attending physician that the baby had gastroschisis, where their abdominal wall had failed to close in utero, resulting in their intestines growing on the outside of their body.

Our charge nurse who took the call – Deanna – said that the woman had presented to A&E with extreme abdominal pain and blood loss, having received no prior care for her pregnancy. She was full-term and, as far as they could ascertain, she hadn't had so much as a blood test or a fetal growth scan. Nobody, including her, had any idea about the baby's birth defect.

"Talking with the mother and father indicated she's from the travelling community, living in a site not too far from the hospital she presented herself to when the blood loss started. Apparently she'd given birth to their four other children by home delivery, only this time she knew something was wrong – not only is she bleeding, but she's several weeks early," said Deanna.

Hurst and Bellamy had joined us by now, and were taking in the information.

"Could be a simple case – could be an operation," I said, holding my hands on my hips as I considered our options. "We won't really know the state of play until we get a look at the baby."

"Will we prepare a spot in ICU?" asked Dr Bellamy.

"Not necessarily," I said. "If the baby is otherwise stable and healthy, we can take our time and keep the trauma to a minimum. If they require ICU, we may need to fix the issue faster."

"She's had absolutely no scans whatsoever until this point?" asked Dr Hurst. "We've no more information than that?"

"None whatsoever," said Deanna. "Have fun with that. Oh, and Dr Hartcliffe?"

"What do you need?"

"I've a maintenance man in to look at the refrigerator in the medicine room – something's up with it. It's been blinking in and out for a while now, but yesterday we had to dispose of ten rounds of insulin," she said.

"That thing's as old as the hills," I said. "But that's an expensive problem. We could do without replacing it right now."

"I'm hoping he can fix it. I'll let you know," said

Deanna.

We met our patient from the helipad, ready to wheel her straight down to surgery. The team had partially sedated her to ease the pain, but she was groaning into her oxygen mask on arrival. We rushed her through the darkness to the backdrop of thrumming helicopter wings, taking advice from the attending paramedics of what treatment she had already received.

While Dr Hurst and Dr Bellamy et all prepared the patient in the OR, I washed my hands and arms thoroughly, getting in deep under the fingernails. As I gloved up and raised my arms to be helped into my gown, I came eye-to-eye with Nina. She held up my gown, her dark eyes studying me, as if looking for clues.

I held my breath, willing myself not to say anything, though I was immediately conflicted with emotions that challenged one another, snapping and snarling. A huge part of me despised Nina for holding such a secret from me, and as time went on, that feeling only festered away. Another, equally large part of me wanted to tear off her scrubs and take her on the next available gurney.

"How's my daughter?" I muttered behind my mask.

"You could find out for yourself," said Nina, making her way behind me to tie up the gown. "The offer was there. Still is."

"I need time." I hissed. "Time to – to figure this all out."

"You found time to fuck me, though, right?" she asked, coming full circle to stand before me, her eyes like two dark stones.

"What do you expect from me? Sense? A single coherent thought? Finding out that – that that little girl is mine – it's fucked with my head, Nina." I could barely believe it was me, ranting and raving, losing my cool – yet I couldn't help myself.

"And what did you expect from me? I was thousands of miles away, scared, alone – and you didn't want kids. Oh, and how about the fact that I barely knew you?"

"I still had a right to know."

"Well now you do." Nina leaned in close, meeting my anger with her own.

Somebody cleared their throat. "Dr Hartcliffe? We're ready for you." Dr Bellamy hovered in the doorway to the sterile theatre, holding up his gloved hands.

"Right you are," I said, switching modes. I glanced back at Nina. "To be continued."

♥

The patient, Moyra, was sedate and stable, and the caesarean section was a success. The bleeding, we found, with the help of the obstetric team, was placental abruption – Moyra was incredibly lucky that we were able to rescue her and the baby in time, before the lack of oxygen killed the baby, and the blood loss killed her.

Moyra was wheeled away for her own recovery while we weighed and examined the baby; a little girl, to be named Niamh. Her intestines were indeed on the outside of her body, and our job was to safely get them back in. First, we needed to catheterise her, warm her up on a heated table, and assess the situation.

"Hurst, tell me: what are the three risks to be observed where gastroschisis is concerned?"

"Number one, sepsis. Two, hypothermia. Three..."

I raised my eyebrows and watched Hurst, waiting. She knew this. She should know this.

"Hypovolemia, reduced sodium in the blood."

"Good. Bellamy – what can you observe about the status of the bowel?"

"Uh – I'm – I'm seeing no necrosis, minimal-to-no signs of VPD."

"What's VPD?"

"Viscero-peritoneal disproportion," said Bellamy. "Kinking in the bowel, swelling, damage –"

"Good. Now on examining Niamh, I can see no reason why we shouldn't proceed with a staged closure – why?"

Dr Bellamy stuttered while Dr Hurst closed her eyes and thought. She opened them abruptly. "Because a slower closure allows for a procedure without the use of anaesthesia and associated risks, a reduced risk of re-operation, and delivers the best general patient recovery and cosmetic outcomes."

"What about our risk of sepsis? How will we manage that?"

"We'll observe routine dressing changes and run a course of antibiotics."

"And why is staging a good approach for Niamh instead of performing a primary closure?"

"Because we've no need to immediately operate. If we did, we would put her at risk of developing complications or undergoing surgical trauma," said Dr Bellamy, rescuing himself at the last moment.

"Good, good. That sounds like a plan to me – nice and gentle," I said.

Lexie's father's words entered my head; when he'd called me a butcher. The spiteful bastard. Very rarely did I let anybody get to me, but that accusation had stung. Never, would I ever, put my infants in any danger of unnecessary risk. Certainly, I wouldn't operate unless it was the best option for their survival.

But it fucking hurt to hear it, nonetheless.

"Now, who wants to fetch me a sterile bag and some gauze rolls? We're going to make ourselves a little silo and let gravity do its work," I said.

Nina set about gathering the appropriate equipment, while Dr Hurst began administering

Niamh's pain relief. At only 36 weeks gestation, her doses would be minimal, but effective in ensuring she was as comfortable as possible.

"Dr Hartcliffe?" asked Dr Bellamy.

"What is it?"

"I'd like to volunteer to apply the sutures, if I may?"

"You may volunteer, but we won't be using sutures. Modern procedures are sutureless, providing a kinder cosmetic appearance on healing," I said, having seen some impressive outcomes myself on my travels.

"How many of these cases have you seen, Ma – I mean – Dr Hartcliffe?" Nina had returned with the bag and gauze, and placed the items on the tray beside me. She seemed to read my mind.

"I see around ten to twelve cases a year," I said. "A few in Sacred Heart, others when I've attended other UK hospitals. A few when I demonstrated in Ukraine. It's a fairly common birth defect. There was a time when it resulted in almost certain death, but with today's procedures, it is almost always certain survival. Luckily for Niamh, she was born in the twenty-first-century."

Nina gently prodded her gloved finger into Niamh's tiny hand while I set about demonstrating the sterilising and bagging of Niamh's intestines. We would be creating a silo, which would gather the intestine above the open abdominal wall and allow gravity to gently return the bowel to the body cavity where it belonged. We could eventually then, very neatly, sew Niamh up and leave her with a very small, neat scar around her belly button.

Though I was entirely unfazed by the procedure, and Hurst and Bellamy were fascinated and eager to contribute, I sensed Nina's unease.

"How are we doing, nurse?" I asked in a gruff voice. I didn't want to let on to my juniors that I was being any more considerate than usual.

"I was just thinking...what a difficult way for a little one to begin her life," said Nina. "I mean, relatively speaking."

I was surprised to hear Nina making the case so personal, taking it to heart. She was a seasoned neonatal nurse. She knew better than that.

"I've seen a lot worse," I said. "Try seeing brain –"

Dr Hurst loudly cleared her throat, and I took the hint. For whatever reason, Nina was feeling particularly emotional about this baby. I needed to lighten the mood. I recalled a song my grandmother used to sing to me when I fell, skimmed my knees, and needed a plaster.

"Sometimes I like to sing my neonates a little song while I work," I said, manipulating the gauze to lift the intestines and get an accurate position for bagging. "The foot bone's connected to the – *leg bone*."

All three glanced up at me in a way that made

me chuckle, as if I'd gone senile.

"Come on, you miserable sods. You know how it goes. Let's give Niamh a nice welcome with the skeleton song. The leg bone's connected to the – ?"

"Knee-bone," sang Bellamy. Kiss-arse – I knew he'd be first.

"The knee bone's connected to the –?"

"Thigh-bone," sang Nina, visibly relaxing.

"The thigh bone's connected to the –"

"Hip bone!" We all sang together, at full volume.

As we completed the song, dissolving into casual laughter, the weight of the atmosphere lifted. Nina's brow unknitted itself and her eyes sparkled as we worked, giving me a feeling of ease. I hadn't realised that my chest had been getting tighter ever since I'd recognised Nina's concern for the baby.

Within the hour, Niamh was patched up and ready to be taken back to nursery room one, where she would make her gentle and safe recovery – complete with her bag of intestines suspended above her tiny body. Her mother was in for a surprise – but, I hoped, it would be a good one.

# CHAPTER THIRTEEN

♥

*Nina*

I tied my hair back in a ponytail and admonished myself in the locker-room mirror. *For goodness' sake, you're a neonatal nurse – why are you getting so involved with every little baby you see and care for? Why are you letting their problems hit so close to home?*

Something was up with me. All right, I was a sensitive person, always had been – it's why I wanted to become a healthcare practitioner in the first place. I believe in having a heart, and I believe in using it to help others. But disallowing my work from distracting me emotionally was something I thought I'd mastered long ago, and now, the problem was resurfacing.

Becoming tearful over our NICU babies when they had a perfectly fixable condition, a great prognosis, and a long healthy life to look forward to? That was a good path to take if I wanted to dissolve into a state of total burnout, and fast.

It wasn't right at all. I picked my face in the mirror – my skin was threatening to break out. I'm emotional, I'm zitty – yikes. When was the last time I'd suffered acne and a case of the blues? *Well, probably when I was pregnant with Maxina*, I thought.

Oh s-h-i-t.

My birth control. I could see it in my mind's eye, still sitting in its paper bag in my bedside drawer, waiting for me to resume my sex life. But I hadn't planned on resuming my sex life – not for a long while, or not until it really, really felt right to.

And it had felt right. So right. When it came to the bedroom, Max had never felt wrong.

But as I began to sweat and realise the danger I could be in – danger that was too late to fix with a morning-after pill now – I gave myself a pep talk.

*It'll be all right. It was only once – no, twice – and you likely weren't even ovulating. Your period is due in one week, and it happened a week ago, so…oh, lord.*

*All right, so you would have been in the danger zone when you had sex. In fact, that's probably why you were so receptive to his advances. You still probably missed the gap by at least a few days, right? People try for years to get pregnant, even when they ovulate regularly. The egg sits around waiting for insemination for 24-48 hours, tops. What makes you think lightning will have struck twice?*

I breathed deep through my nostrils and let out

a long breath through my mouth. Then I did it again, and again, until I felt myself calming down. Either my period would come in a week or so, right on schedule, or I would take a test and...well, then I'd know.

Until then, I had a little girl to get home to.

I shrugged on my brown suede jacket and made for the elevators. If I got home fairly quickly, I would have time for a cup of tea and some peace and quiet before I needed to wake my daughter and mother up. The five-til-five shift was a killer, but I'd taken it on because I needed the extra hours – money was getting pretty tight. I made my way out into the darkness, my breath leaving my mouth in a fine mist. It was a crisp early morning, with very little traffic on the roads. Birds chirped as they flitted against the navy blue sky, hopping between the branches of the trees lining the walkway to the entrance of the hospital.

All that early-morning Hampstead beauty, and I felt that someone was coming after me. I sensed them first, and then I heard their footsteps. Would anybody hear me if I screamed at this hour?

"Nina?"

I knew that voice. It was Max.

I spun around to face him; he was dressed in his coat and scarf, looking rough, worn, and gruffly handsome. He also looked like he could do with some help ironing his clothes, but hey – he was a busy man. I could hardly blame him when I spent most of my shifts covered in milk spatters and poop.

"Nina, wait for me," he said, hastening into a jog. "I need a word with you."

I sighed as he caught up with me, shaking my head. "A whole week and you've barely spoken to me about Maxina. I'm beginning to wish you'd never found out."

"You don't mean that. I had a right to know."

"I had a right to my privacy," I said, knowing I was being unfair – but it was how I truly felt. "Now things are all messed up and awkward between us. One moment you couldn't get enough of me, and you seemed almost happy about Maxina, and the next –"

"Give me a break, Nina. I've just found out I'm a father to a fourteen-month-old child. Your child. Fuck, *our* child! You didn't mind keeping it a secret all that time – at least give me a courtesy period of a week or so to take the bloody news in," said Max.

"I did mind," I said, looking down at the toes of my boots. "It ate away at me, but I was thousands of miles away and you...were here."

"Out of sight, out of mind?"

I looked up, meeting his eyes with mine. "Never."

Max glanced around at the empty streets, pocketing his hands in his coat. "Look, none of that matters now. I think it's important that we communicate – try and figure out a way forward."

*And what about me and you?* I wanted to ask – but I think he was making that perfectly clear by not addressing it. An impassioned quickie in the bunk room did not require strings, apparently; my status as the mother of his child notwithstanding. He was recently engaged; what could I expect, other than to be his rebound, when he was in a state of shock as well as in the midst of a break-up?

"And how do you suppose we do that?" I asked.

"We sit down, like two grown-ups, and we come up with a plan," said Max. "Let me take you for a coffee right now and go over a few things."

I chuckled, holding up my arms and spinning around to demonstrate the emptiness of our surroundings. "Coffee? Look around you – there's nothing open at this hour."

"There is," said Max, tapping his nose. "If you're in the know. There's a place just around the corner arranging their morning pastries as we speak. Follow me."

Max strode away with his hands in his pockets, and I found myself looking after him with my eyebrows raised. I guess I sprinted out of work and back home so soon after my shifts ended that I'd never even bothered to get to know the area – definitely not to the degree that I knew of any early-morning coffee bars. Hampstead Village had a beautiful, sleepy, small-town-feel, with the sprawling heath not far away. The leafy streets and gently glowing lampposts certainly had a fairytale feel about them at this time in the morning, and I found the prospect of stopping to enjoy it quite alluring.

It would at least make the awkwardness between us more bearable if we confronted one another with a coffee in-hand amongst cosy surroundings.

I found myself hurrying after Max, muttering out loud that I could only spare thirty-minutes, tops. I had a long bus journey to make.

"It won't be a problem," said Max, when I caught up with him. "I'll drop you home."

*Yes*, I thought. *I remember how that turned out last time.* At least this time my mother and daughter were home, sleeping – I wouldn't be liable to give in to any sudden whims with them around.

Max took us to a place on the corner with arched wood-framed windows and garlands of evergreen foliage hanging from them like an Italienté garden. The shop inside glowed orange as if lit by a crackling fireplace, with its warmth flooding out onto the pavement. Scents of coffee and warm cinnamon rolls wafted over us as we approached the door. A sign above the shop in a swirling wrought-iron frame simply said *Gina's*.

A member of staff in a crisp pinafore was setting up chairs and tables outside, while another swept the fallen leaves into the road with a wooden broomstick.

"This is my favourite place to come and spend some time," said Max, holding the door for me. As I stepped over the threshold, a bell gently rang out above our heads. Inside were café-style tables with wooden chairs and sheepskin throws arranged around what was, to my surprise, an actual glowing fireplace. There were cosy nooks with booths and bookshelves lined with leather-bound classics, and each table was dressed with a simple white candle in an open-top glass.

It was refreshing – comforting, even – to see Max in this environment instead of the sterile units and long, dull halls of the hospital. Even our ward, Little Neptune, with its colours and children's paintings and the great sea life mural on the foyer wall, seemed clinical compared to this. Here, Max seemed warmer, softer; dare I say, boyfriend material.

Max found us a booth in the corner, closer to the fireplace, and gestured for me to sit in first. I would be snuggled in so far that I wouldn't be able to leave quickly if I needed to, and that made me uneasy. I didn't know how well this conversation was going to go. Before I could object, Max shrugged off his coat and hung it over the chair opposite the booth, indicating he was taking his place there, rather than beside me. I relaxed a little and slid into the booth. I took off my jacket and laid it beside me, but Max indicated I should pass it to him with a wave. He hung my coat up on a nearby antique rack, before unwinding his scarf and laying it over my coat.

He was being calm, thoughtful, considerate – not barking orders like he did back on the ward. He was taking care of me.

"This is really beautiful," I said, taking it all in. The coffee bar was alive with a steaming espresso machine. Baskets of freshly baked pastries and plaited breads were being brought out from the kitchen and displayed on the counter in the style of a farmer's market.

"What can I get you?" asked Max. "My treat. I'm having an Americano."

"No, no, it's all right – I can pay for my own – "

"Nina," said Max in a flat voice. "It's a pastry and a coffee. You can let me treat you to that, surely?"

I'd treated him to a whole lot more, but the thought of it now made me blush. I ducked my head, pretending to forage in my backpack, to hide my shame.

"Thanks, that'd be lovely," I mumbled. "I'll have a hot chocolate and a...a er..."

Max was smiling as if amused by something. He wore a faded plaid shirt over a white T-shirt; the plaid looked as if it might have been red at some point. He rolled his sleeves up to the elbows and held out his hand to me.

"Shall we have a look at what they've got?"

Without thinking, I took his hand and let him

guide me to the coffee bar. We held hands longer than I intended, but it felt too rude to abruptly pull away. At some point our hands fell away from one another and I folded my arms under my breast, not knowing what to do with myself. I noticed Max pocketed his hands, cleared his throat, and frowned at the menus scribbled in chalk.

Max ordered our drinks, and asked for an apple turnover for himself. An apple turnover! I looked away and snorted, trying – and failing – to stifle my laughter.

"What?" he asked.

"I'm sorry," I said, unable to hold off the fit of giggles that came over me. "I just never saw you eating dainty pastries."

He smiled a wry smile, stroking the stubble on his jaw. "I'm a man of many mysteries," he said. "I'm glad you find me so amusing, Ms Dorrington."

The way he said my name gave me shivers, but I focused my eyes on the pastries and breads, forcing any thoughts like that away. We were here to talk business, and it was beginning to feel...well, like a date.

Like a cosy coffee date with a hunky surgeon, who was pretty much my boss.

I groaned, acting as though I was struggling to choose something to eat, when really I was complaining about myself and my insane libido and near insatiable awkwardness. Just the sight of Max's furry forearms and large hands folded at his chest was enough to make my belly flip-over, and that's without the sexy plaid shirt.

"Can I suggest an apricot Danish?" Max whispered, nudging me with his arms still folded.

"No, no," I said, training my eyes on the baskets of goods. "I can do this." *Just pick something, you idiot.* "I'll have a cinnamon roll," I said finally, watching the barista select it on the screen with a relieved smile.

Max took out his wallet – *who the heck paid with their actual card, instead of using a pay app on their phone, in this day and age*?! – and I automatically began to object.

"Shut yer pie-hole, Nina," he said. "This is on me. Go and sit down before you give me the hump."

I sighed, taking my seat back at the booth. I watched him pay with his bank card and chuckled into my fist, shaking my head. When Max returned with our tray of goodies and steaming mugs, he noticed my smirk and rolled his eyes.

"What embarrassing thing have I done now?"

I snorted, nearly making him spill his Americano.

"A bank card, Max?"

He frowned. "I know I don't leave the hospital a right lot, but as far as I know, that's still a legitimate payment method. I just used it, didn't I?"

He passed me my cinnamon roll – still warm,

with a sticky glaze – and I took a bite straight into it. My teeth sank into marshmallowy, brown-sugar laden goodness; as I tore my bite away, a little steam gently wafted from its insides, filling my senses with scents of apples and cinnamon.

I swallowed the bite and felt it nourishing me instantly. "If you pass me your phone, I could show you how to download the right app, upload your virtual bank card, and you can pay with that. It's much easier. Who do you bank with?"

"None of your business, you cheeky mare. A man's entitled to his privacy, you know," said Max, blowing the steaming surface of his coffee. Then he reached into his pocket and tossed his phone across the table toward me. "Oh bugger it, go on then. I don't usually bother with change. I'm a bit older than you, in case you didn't notice."

"Not that much older," I said, picking up the phone.

His home screen was an old photograph of a man and a woman at the beach. The man was holding up a little boy, and they were all smiling, squinting against the glare of the sun. They looked content and happy. The little boy was holding what looked like a plastic dinosaur.

"Who's that?" I asked.

"That's my mother and father – both getting on quite a bit now, I'm afraid – and that's me there, in my best trunks," said Max. "That little fellow in my hand is Fluffy."

I grinned, taking in the photo, imagining Max as an innocent little boy. I focused on his face, the way his eyes reflected the sunlight, so pale in colour it was as if they were transparent. My heart pounded when I realised I recognised that face. It was just like Maxina's.

I slid the phone back across the table, suddenly feeling guilt-ridden and panicked. I picked up my mug of hot chocolate and blew around the whipped cream, knowing it was still far too hot to drink, but needing to do something – anything – with my hands.

"I'll do it another time, actually, Max. We've got more important things to discuss," I said abruptly. He paused before pocketing his phone.

"Right, right. Of course. You're right." Max cleared his throat. "And we don't have too much time before I need to be getting you home. All right – seeing as you mentioned payments, I might as well show you the real reason I brought you here tonight – or this morning, rather. I'm afraid you're going to roll your eyes again – it's old fashioned."

I frowned as he took an envelope out of his coat pocket and, using his thumb and two fingers, pulled out a long, thin, slip of paper.

Max drew in a deep breath and let it out in a sigh.

"This is a cheque, Nina. It's what I feel I owe you for your – for our – daughter. I've calculated all your nursery fees, clothing, maintenance, travel expenses...well, you name it. It all started to get rather complicated, so forgive me if it's not exact. What it is, is a start. That's all. A start at putting things right."

He slid the cheque across the table to me with two fingers. My eyes bulged when I saw the carefully written number in blue ink, spelled out beneath it in the most beautiful – and surprising – cursive handwriting.

"You can't be serious," I said, my voice faltering. "That's – that's twenty thousand pounds."

"It's what I owe you at least," said Max. "Now don't get me wrong, Nina – I'm angry. God knows I'm angry. But I'm trying to think first of that little girl, and what we need to be doing for her. I haven't played my part – the reasons for that don't matter. All right, they do – but not right now. Christ – look, Nina, I've messed this up. I don't do speeches. Just do me a favour and take the money, all right?"

I frowned, looking up from the cheque to him. "But what does this mean? You're not – you're not just paying me a flat fee and walking away?"

Max smiled down at his coffee, surprising me. And there I was, with my hackles rising, ready to give him hell.

"No. Not by a long shot. It's a start, that's all. A start at making things equal – at co-parenting. Now, I know things have been a bit…confusing."

"You could say that," I said.

"But they don't have to be. We can keep this pure; keep this simple. I think we can make a go of it, you and me," said Max, covering my hand with his. I began to melt, instantly, and found it hard to piece any words together.

"W-what would that look like, exactly? You and me?"

Max squeezed my hand. "Co-parenting, 50/50. I provide and look after you both financially – that's a start, right? – and...I don't know. We start with play dates, let Maxina meet me; let her get more comfortable with me. Days at the park. Anything you need, I'm there. Anything she needs, I'm there. I want to be the father she deserves, and the support that you deserve."

I nodded slowly, noticing that he made no mention of us – no mention of how *we* would interact going forward.

"You want us to be grown up about this," I said. "But there's just one problem with that."

"What problem?"

"I'm not a prostitute. You could have given me the cheque without screwing my brains out," I said, sliding it back across the table to him.

He stabbed it with his fingers and slid it right back.

"Nina, take the money. This isn't about me and you."

"Isn't it?"

"No, it isn't. If it was, you'd have damn-well called me from Kampala the minute you discovered you were pregnant with Maxina," said Max, struggling to keep his voice hushed. Early morning commuters were beginning to filter into the store, making their coffee orders.

I saw, now, that he was hurt as well as angry underneath – that he was keeping calm and kind because he was *being a grown up*. That knowledge only irritated me. That, and the fact he was right – about everything. I *had* withheld the information. I'd treated him like he didn't matter. Why, then, did I find myself longing for him to address the elephant in the room when it came to me and him getting physical? We had much, much bigger problems than that.

"So this whole screwing-my-brains-out thing that happened a week ago – what is that, some kind of pressure release for you?" I asked. "Because I struggle to understand that level of intimacy versus the anger I'm seeing in your eyes right now, Max."

He frowned down at his coffee as he took a long sip.

"That's one way of putting it," he said. "I was infuriated. I was – I was mixed up. Look, I'm trying to make things right. I'm trying to fix this."

"Me and my daughter aren't broken," I said. "And if we're really being as clinical as this about it, then I don't want your hands anywhere near me again. That's all I wanted to make clear."

Even as I said those words, I knew I didn't mean

them. I wanted Max. I wanted his hands very much all over me. But I couldn't allow myself to fall for him while he acted as though he could pay his way into our lives, or set up some artificial scenario where we acted like we hadn't had hot, confusing sex.

"Fine," said Max with an irritated tone. "That's fine by me."

His coldness hit me like a slap to the face, but I remained calm – for Maxina's sake, we really did need to figure something out.

"Good," I said.

We paused, avoiding one another's eye-line as we sipped our drinks. Without realising, I had torn my cinnamon roll up into shreds.

"So you'll take the cheque, then, yes?" asked Max in a clipped tone, still not meeting my gaze. His eyes stared off into the crackling fireplace while he awaited my response.

"Sure," I said, picking it up from the table – as if holding up a dead mouse by its tail – and depositing it in my backpack.

"Good. And we'll...we'll arrange a schedule for me to see Maxina?"

I softened a little as he said that, feeling secure in the knowledge, at least, that he really did want to see her – that he really did have fatherly love for her that could blossom and grow.

"Of course," I said.

Max smiled a half-smile, his mouth forming a neutral line. "We can do this, Nina. I'm confident of that. You and I work too well in the operating room for that not to be the case. If we can handle fragile lives together, then we can raise a child together."

I swallowed a sip of my now lukewarm hot chocolate, realising I'd missed the best of it by letting it cool for too long.

"Maybe we can," I said, matching his neutral smile.

Inside, I was screaming, asking questions I couldn't understand myself. *Why do you see me as a co-parent and not a lover, a partner?*

But he had made himself clear, and, I guessed, so had I. My actions in hiding Maxina's existence – whatever my excuses may have been – were just too immoral for him to overlook. I would have to accept that in my own time. What was the phrase my mother always used? I'd made my bed – and now, I would have to lie in it.

♥

It was almost daylight when we arrived outside my flat. I could tell by the way the curtains were drawn that my mother and Maxina were still sleeping.

On the journey over – one that we took in a contemplative silence – I reflected on my decision to conceal Maxina. Fear had been my motivator; a fear that he would reject her. But it had been wrong nonetheless, and there could be no justification for it.

I would have to work just as hard as Max to make it up somehow. As I unbuckled my seatbelt, I thought of the first step I could take.

"Come inside," I said. "Come and see her."

Max looked uncertainly up at the apartment window. "I couldn't. She's sleeping. No, no, another time."

I took Max's hand and squeezed it. "Max. Come upstairs and see your daughter."

We tip-toed to Maxina's room at the end of the hall, making sure to be extra careful going past the living room where my mother slept on my fold-out bed. I was impressed by Max's ability to be so gentle and graceful despite his size, but then again, didn't he perform that particular magic every time he operated?

I gently opened Maxina's room and guided Max to her crib, where she lay snuggled with her stuffed toy rabbit. Her baby face was relaxed in sleep, her eyelashes fluttering as she dreamed. Max paused, taking her in. I saw how his eyes lingered on her cherubic face and fell over her neck where her curls were damp with sleep-sweat. How they drifted over her hands, fanned out, displaying her perfect fingers.

Max's breathing had become slightly ragged, and I could tell he wanted to cry. Instinctively – despite my assertion that our hands would not touch one another – my arm wrapped around his waist, wanting to reassure him. His arm immediately encircled my shoulders and he bowed his head to meet mine. I found myself welling with tears, and we held each other tighter.

We were mum and dad, overlooking our sleeping daughter. From that perspective, at least –

I knew things were going to be okay.

# CHAPTER FOURTEEN
♥

*Max*

Dr Hurst ambushed me almost immediately as I entered the locker room. She looked wild with urgency, her sandy-coloured hair flying about her head as she grabbed me by the arm.

"Jennifer, what the heck is wrong with you? Are you all right?" I asked as she held onto my arm for dear life. She seemed almost out of breath.

"I ran here as soon as I – " she wheezed, leaning against a locker for support. I was getting close to offering her an inhaler. "God, Max – I don't even know how to tell you."

I frowned at her, getting annoyed now.

"You can start by spitting it out," I said, folding my arms. "I don't think I need to tell you just how manic the next few hours is going to be, do I? We need to be getting scrubbed-in pronto."

Several children had been flown in as emergency cases with all manner of catastrophic injuries, and they were being prepared for surgery as we spoke. A bus had turned over on its way to a school field-trip; there'd been a fire. Although all of the children survived, several had crushed their limbs, while others had suffered burns. Some had suffered both. There were simply too many of them for their local hospitals to cope with, and some of the most serious cases were being transferred to us.

It would be all hands on deck from every available medic hospital-wide at Sacred Heart, and we would be pushed to capacity.

"She – she was in London for the big conference –"

"What? Who?"

"Just listen! Oh god, Max –"

The door to the locker room swung open.

Dr Hurst and I turned to glance at the woman standing in the doorway, wearing a pencil skirt and killer heels.

"Oh fucking hell," I said under my breath.

"If it isn't my handsome ex-fiancé," said Hannah Shepherd in her devilish accent, smiling like a cat who'd spied a mouse. "I'll be damned!"

Dr Hurst hesitated by my side, as if she wasn't sure whether to defend me or run and hide. My colleagues had been dismayed to hear of my decision to end the relationship, but I'd given no details – only that we were through. The assumption, I guessed, had been that Hannah had betrayed me in some way, or else why would we split so soon after becoming engaged? But I'd been keen to move on and let sleeping dogs lie, so I'd never explained a damn thing to them. All I'd wanted was to move on.

The details hadn't mattered when I thought I wasn't going to see her again – why would I explain anything if she was never stepping foot on my ward again? But now she was here, looking jaw-droppingly gorgeous with her long, white-blonde hair and crystal blue eyes. The staff were going to have fun whispering about this.

"Dr Shepherd. What are you doing here?"

Hannah cocked a wry smile, folding her arms under her large bust. They were designer breasts that she'd been particularly proud of, and I – admittedly – had been quite the fan of them too. Now that I thought of her bare chest, I felt uncomfortable, wrong. Imagining us together like that seemed bizarre to me now. Yet by any man's standards, she was the absolute dream: a super-genius with legs like a supermodel and an award-winning career in plastics and re-constructive surgery. I should have considered myself lucky.

Why, then, did I now feel like the only luck I'd had was to make a lucky *escape*?

"Dr Shepherd, now? I guess we are back to simple formalities. Max told you we broke up, right Dr Hurst?"

Jennifer's mouth dropped open and she looked

like a frightened little lamb, glancing between me and Hannah.

"I'm – I'm going to scrub in. Dr Bellamy said there's a – a – a leg re-attachment happening in OR2," said Dr Hurst. "I'd better get over there."

As she fled the locker room, Hannah called over her shoulder. "I'll see you there, Dr Hurst. I believe that one has my name on it."

"You're here for the bus crash?" I asked. "Who called you?"

"The chief executive herself," said Hannah. "It's going to be one hell of a freak show around here if they don't get some serious re-constructive support on the case, don't you think? They're lucky I happened to be in London."

"You don't think things will be a bit – you know – awkward between the two of us?" I asked, still baffled to see her there before me in the flesh. It had been impossible to get her here when we were engaged, and now that we'd split, here she was. "I mean – you don't think it'll get in the way of our work?"

"Not unless you think so," said Hannah. "Come on, Max. We're professionals."

I was relieved to hear that. In the brief time I'd known Hannah, I'd gotten used to her penchant for drama, knowing how she could behave if things didn't go her way. There'd be no room for that now, and I needed to know that she was going to behave herself.

"I'm glad to hear it," I said.

"And besides, you're the one *I* should be worrying about. When you don't get your own way, you can be a real big baby," said Hannah. "I haven't forgotten about your little tantrums on the ward when staff pissed you off, or if your surgeries got rescheduled against your wishes."

She was grinning with her impossibly white teeth, her pumped-up lips curling up in an impish grin.

"You what? You cheeky so-and-so – I'm the professional here, out of the two of us," I said, feeling slightly stung. She had witnessed some of my worst moments. At one point, I'd considered that evidence of our tight bond – now, it was only evidence of my embarrassment.

"I'm just stating the facts. You're the one who asked if I was capable of keeping things professional. The question is – can you?" Hannah stepped toward me until she was inches from my face. Her eyes studied mine.

Not long ago, she would have driven me wild just by being that close to me. I stepped around her, aiming for the door.

"Come on," I said, holding the door open for her. "We've got work to do."

♥

Hannah kept to her word, at least – she was the absolute professional, and I had faith that we could at least get through this disaster together.

We worked like a well-oiled machine on several surgeries, until we were exhausted. The whole hospital was pulling out all the stops to ensure these primary school children were patched up like so many broken dolls.

Hannah's eyes were focused and determined as she instructed our gaggle of interns and experienced colleagues, everyone pitching in. She was the glamorous enigma among us, wowing them all with her expert sutures that were so small and neat that they looked to be woven by mice.

These children would have fully-functioning limbs and barely even a scar to show for their trouble. Despite our differences, my respect was renewed for Hannah, and I felt that we had at least achieved some closure.

That is, until she followed me from the OR, asking to have a word.

"I'd love to catch up, Hannah, but I've got to get myself some fresh air," I said, pulling off my surgical cap and running my hand through my hair. "We've another three scheduled this afternoon."

"Oh come on, we're over the worst of it. A few skin grafts and a burns treatment won't push us over the edge, will they?"

I gave her a look that made her throw back her head in sunny laughter. She was on a high from one successful surgery after another; I knew that feeling. But this time I wasn't the superstar, she was – and she was loving the chance to show off.

"Maybe not, but I still need my fresh air," I said, heading back to Little Neptune for the locker room.

"Perfect," said Hannah, hurrying after me in her flat, hospital-appropriate shoes. "I'll come with you. I've got a proposition that I think you'll want to hear."

I stopped in my tracks, frowning. "What are you talking about?"

She smiled warmly at me, taking me by surprise. What did Hannah have to feel warm about when it came to me?

"Wait and see," she said.

♥

We came to a stop at the bottom of the moss-covered stone steps. After a gentle tour around Hampstead Heath gardens, Hannah was finally getting to the point of our little sojourn.

"I'll cut to the chase. John still wants you, Max. He wants you to join our Children's hospital, put a whole campaign behind you to boost your profile, the works. Our break-up was a huge disappointment to him. He thought we'd be the dynamic couple. He was willing to put real money behind us to boost our image, make the hospital look like the best in the world." Hannah was speaking rapidly, clearly excited.

"But we're not together," I said. "So how can he still want me there?"

John Reed was the CEO of Hannah's base hospital in Los Angeles. He made all their big-budget decisions and arranged his top surgeons between several hospitals the way a football manager arranged his players. It was strictly business.

"That's the beauty of it," said Hannah, her eyes lighting up. "We don't have to be a real couple. We can pretend. If we present ourselves as that power couple we thought we'd be, what difference will it really make? We can still work together. We've proven that."

"Hannah, that's just crazy," I said. "You want to create a marriage of convenience?"

"Not necessarily. Well, maybe. Would that be so wrong?"

"I don't intend to live a lie," I said. "This commercial crap doesn't appeal to me."

"Would millions of dollars appeal to you? Would a career in TV appeal to you? How about the chance to save children's lives and actually see some financial *reward* for it?"

She had a point there, maybe. We hardly earned a king's ransom in the UK, and we rarely got the recognition we deserved. When parents were disappointed in me, or didn't trust me, it did get to me. At least where Hannah was coming from, there were aspects that sweetened the deal somewhat.

But, that is *not* why I became a children's doctor.

"I got into this game to make sure our newborn babies have the best chance at a healthy start in life," I said, pacing the stone paving. "I'm not here for any other reason."

"You can work neonatal in LA. You can be the hero. You can have it *all*. Come on, Max – what's keeping you here?"

Hannah took a step toward me, reaching out her hand. Her fingertips brushed my face, before trailing through my hair. Her eyes studied mine.

"Were we really too distant, Max? Was it really such a bad idea?" She raised her other hand and held my jaw, letting her fingers run over my stubble. "Can't I persuade you?"

Hannah pressed her lips against mine, tipping her head to one side. She pressed her impressive bust against my chest as she kissed me, and I found my arms encircling her waist. She moaned softly as our mouths parted, making way for her tongue to glide and caress my own.

Before we broke up, that kiss would have sent my libido sky high, and I would have had to take her against a damn tree somewhere. Her body would have driven me wild, her lips teasing me, her breasts sending me rock hard.

But I felt nothing. Absolutely nothing.

Hannah knew it, too. She pulled away, blinking, with questions in her eyes.

"There's something you need to know," I said, ready to admit the truth. "After we split – and please believe me, it was *after* we split – I discovered that I...well, I'm a father."

Hannah took a step back, shaking her head in confusion. "What? How can that be?"

"It's a long story. Forgive me if I preserve my child's privacy, but...suffice it to say, it was a shock when I found out. She was the result of a very brief fling some time ago, and now...well, I'm going to do the right thing."

"The right thing would be to take your career to the next level," said Hannah. "To make real money – to support the child."

She didn't sound entirely convinced of her own idea there.

"I want to get to know my child, Hannah. Surely you can understand that?"

She wrinkled her nose as if in disgust. "You're wasting yourself, Max. Can't *you* understand that?"

"I don't expect you to get it, but there it is," I said. "My decision is final. I'm staying in London for good."

Hannah scoffed, shaking her head. "I just hope you don't live to regret this, because this offer won't come around again. I guess...I guess that's it, then."

"That's it," I said.

Hannah rolled her eyes, folding her arms. All the excitement had well and truly left her eyes, leaving them flat and soulless.

"We should get back," she said, turning and hurrying up the stone stairway. I watched her go, feeling no remorse whatsoever. Maxina needed me now.

And, I realised, I needed her.

# CHAPTER FIFTEEN

♥

*Nina*

Hannah Shepherd was thundering my way in her killer heels. Surgeries must have finally been completed, and she was back in her standard *come fuck me* uniform. She held out a signed form and passed it to me, looking me up and down.

"I need you to run this to toxicology for me. I'm waiting for some lab results on one of my bus kids," she said, passing me the urgent request form.

I winced at the phrase – she'd said it in a sing-song way as if she wasn't describing a traumatised child who had nearly lost their life in a crash. Not only that, but a child who had been airlifted hundreds of miles from home to receive their treatment.

"Sure," I said, "I can run this down to the lab on my way out. I'm just finishing up here."

"Great. Thanks." She spun away from me in a

swish of platinum locks.

"Dr Shepherd?" I called after her. She turned, blinking at me as if she'd already forgotten my existence in the few seconds it had taken her to turn away.

"Yes?"

"We don't refer to them as bus kids. That's offensive. If a parent were to overhear you – "

"*Excuse me*?"

I faced her off, knowing that I wasn't overstepping my mark. As a nurse, it was my job to advocate for my patients and their families. I'd dealt with enough arrogant doctors – and the surgeons were the absolute *worst*, Max Hartcliffe included – to know I wasn't afraid of this one.

"Don't call them bus kids, all right?"

Hannah put a hand on her hip and licked her lips, as if preparing to give me a dressing-down. Deanna, our charge nurse, made her slow meander toward us, an eyebrow cocked. She was weighing up the situation.

"Do we have a problem here, nurse? Doctor S?"

Hannah folded her arms. "Your scrub nurse thinks she can tell me what I can and can't say."

I shook my head, giving Deanna the *look*. She slowly closed her eyes and opened them, indicating she was already bored of Dr Shepherd. She knew the score with the doctors – especially visiting surgeons who thought they were making some kind of impression. What they didn't know is that they couldn't surprise us – we'd seen it all. We'd cleaned up more than enough of their mistakes.

"All I'm asking is that you speak politely about our patients. I would not want to do the explaining if a parent were to over-hear you," I said, keeping my voice polite but firm.

Hannah narrowed her eyes, readying to snipe back with something particularly acerbic, I was sure.

"Wait, what did you say, exactly?" Deanna was looking at Hannah now with a stern look that even made her do a double take.

"Bus kids," she said flatly. "I said *bus kids*."

Deanna tapped her in the chest with the print-outs she was holding, looking her directly in the eyes. Deanna was a foster parent as well as a nurse, and she knew how to make a child feel ashamed of their wrongdoing with little more than a look. It was certainly working on Hannah.

"We don't do that here, Dr Shepherd. And nurse Dorrington is a valued neonatal nurse and a scrub nurse. She's respected all across this hospital. Do you understand that?" said Deanna.

Hannah sucked in a long breath through flared nostrils, giving me one lasting look of malice. "Yep," she said, before turning and walking away.

Deanna glanced at me with her eyebrows raised. "Somebody needs to teach that little girl some manners. I've enough problems – we've got four nurses off the reservation and a refrigerator that's determined to break itself. I've got maintenance in again this afternoon. Are you off, now?"

"*Yep*," I said, relaxed now that I knew – once again – that Deanna had my back. "I'm off to see my little girl."

"You give that cherub a hug from me," said Deanna. "And make sure you get yourself some rest too, mama."

As I left the locker room with my bag and coat, I saw Hannah again in the hall, talking to someone inside a doorway. I didn't want to have any more unpleasantness with her, so I made my way to the elevator and pressed the call button several times. As I stepped inside, I watched her leave the room looking flustered, fanning her face as she walked with her notes.

The person who stepped out after her was Max, glancing up and down the hall each way before committing to his exit – as if he was worried about getting caught. Why would he be looking so shifty?

Then it hit me. Hannah had made her move on him. He was being sucked back in. What if she took him to the states with her after all, pulling him away from Maxina for good?

Taking him away from *me*?

♥

Rest! How could I possibly rest with those

questions spinning in my mind?

Fortunately, I had my chance to get answers – Max and I were meeting for our play date, and I would be demanding the truth. As a mother, I didn't have time for any foolishness or mucking around. If Max intended to take up with Hannah again and make a life and career in California after all, then I needed to know.

This understanding of ours, where we respected open communication, had to go both ways.

"Are you looking forward to seeing daddy?" I asked Maxina, leaning over the buggy as I pushed her along. The air was crisp and autumnal, a light breeze winding its way through the park, skimming over the surface of the duck pond.

My stomach was in knots, but I knew I had nothing to worry about. Max had already proved he was a natural with kids – his job notwithstanding – and he clearly felt a bond with Maxina. My question was – how long would this last?

The buggy was one of my first purchases I made with the money Max had given us. Her tatty old pushchair from the children's centre had been loaned out and re-used hundreds of times, and was truly looking its age. Now I was able to give Maxina a new luxury system with plush padding, a muff to cover her legs, and best of all, a coffee cup holder for me.

Now, my baby was going around in style – and so

was I.

"Wow. Nice wheels," said Max, getting up from the bench overlooking the duck pond. He was wearing his long black knitted coat and scarf, his hair tousled from the breeze. "For you," he said, handing me a hot drink in doubled-up cup.

"Thank you," I said, giving it a sniff. "Pumpkin spice?"

"Tis the season," he said. "And for you." He handed Maxina a small carton of apple juice with a bendy straw. She took it with a delighted smile and immediately began sucking down the sugary contents.

He picked up a cup of his own from beneath the bench and we walked, stopping to feed the ducks as we crossed the bridge over the pond. Max took Maxina out of her pushchair and held her up so she could throw handfuls of feed to the waiting birds, including some angry-looking swans and feisty geese who joined the throng.

He continued holding her as we entered the play park, taking her straight to the swings.

"Not too high, all right, daddy?" I said, eliciting a sheepish smile from him on the word *daddy*. He did as he was asked, pushing her very gently – too gently, almost, as if he were afraid of breaking her.

"All right, that's over-kill," I said. "You're going to bore our daughter to death!"

Max pushed a little harder, but only a little – Maxina had fun all the same, kicking out her legs.

"If she falls out and hurts herself, I'll never forgive myself," said Max.

"Take it easy," I said, sipping my warm drink. It was the perfect temperature. "So, I er...I met Hannah Shepherd, briefly. Will you be joining her in the states after all?"

Max frowned as he pushed Maxina. "No," he said, "absolutely not."

"You two aren't back together?"

Max looked at me as if I was talking gibberish, but I wasn't going to let it go. I wanted to know the truth.

"No," he said, with so much emphasis that he seemed almost offended.

I sighed. "I saw you two together, Max. Please. If there's something you need to tell me, then I want to know right now. It'll save us both the grief later on."

Max chuckled. "I am *not* seeing Hannah Shepherd and I am *not* going to the states with her. Jesus, Nina, why would I?"

I hid my face behind a sip of my latté, feeling foolish now.

"Who have you been talking to?" asked Max, a deep frown creasing his brow.

"Nobody," I said, swallowing hard. "I was just...making sure. I don't even know why I would have thought you were getting back together."

"Hey," said Max, reaching out for my elbow and

squeezing it. "I'm not going anywhere, not now. I couldn't."

I held my breath. "Why not?"

"Because my daughter lives here, of course."

"Of course," I said, unsure of what exactly I was hoping to hear. "Good. I'm glad to hear it."

Max sighed. "If you want to know the truth, Hannah did proposition me again. She made all kinds of offers – offers coming from the top. Even some offers coming from *her*. I turned them all down."

"You *did*?" I asked, feeling quite impressed. He had to have turned down a pretty penny…and a lot of other stuff, too.

"I'm serious, Nina. I'm serious about our child. Didn't I make that clear the last time we met?"

"Yes, you did," I said, realising how silly I'd been to second guess him like that. Why *was* I second-guessing him? Why was I behaving in such a possessive, distrusting way?

*Because you're jealous*, a voice in my head said. I shook the thought away, but I knew the voice was telling the truth.

"I don't know if you know this, but I've been somewhat of a free-loader at the hospital for a number of years now," said Max, looking uncomfortable.

Oh, I knew. Of course I knew. Who didn't know that Max literally lived at the hospital, only leaving to catch a few much-needed winks of sleep?

"Well, all that's changing. I've been doing a lot of thinking, Nina. I'm going to get a house in Hampstead." He cleared his throat, looking up at the clouds above us. "I'm going to buy a family home. Somewhere for Maxina to run and play, where she can have a big bedroom."

My heart surged to hear that, but then it stopped. How could my tiny apartment possibly compare to a whopping great house in the Hampstead Garden suburbs?

"Max, that sounds lovely, but...you're not talking about taking custody of Maxina, are you? You're not talking about her living there permanently?"

"Away from you? God, no," said Max. "Jesus, Nina. When are you going to start trusting me, pet?"

I shivered, glad to have nipped that in the bud. "I'm doing my best to provide for my daughter, but it'll be a tough one competing with a house like that," I said, already dreading the conversations I'd be having when she was older – asking me why we didn't live in a grand house like daddy's.

"We're not competing," said Max in a soft voice, looking me in the eyes. I believed him. "We're a team, you and me. We'll have a space for Christmases, birthdays, pool parties...whatever she needs. I won't ever take her away from you. You've already given her more than I could ever pay back."

His sincerity overwhelmed me, and tears pricked my eyes. He lifted Maxina out of the swing and brought her to me. She fit so snugly between us.

"Everything is going to be all right. You'll see." said Max.

I could see that Max had adjusted his way of speaking to me lately, leaving his blunt and brash approach at the door. He'd adopted a softer method that, despite being nowhere near as cutting, was somehow more direct. I decided I would take his word as truthful, now, and stop casting everything he said with a big black cloud of doubt. I owed him that.

Maxina beamed at him, nuzzling her face against his. It was all too right, too perfect. We may not be a traditional family, or even a couple, for heaven's sake – but we were fast becoming a unit. It was more than I could have hoped for.

Max wrapped a comforting arm around me and we held each other, the three of us. All kinds of feelings stirred up inside me, swirling up like leaves.

Could I – should I – cave into them? There was simply no way to. We'd already acted impulsively, broken all protocols, and made our working relationship as tough as humanly possible.

I could only imagine the damage that something like love could do, if I let myself throw that into the mix. The question for me was this:

# did I really have a choice in the matter?

# CHAPTER SIXTEEN
♥

Max

I stopped in the doorway of the family room, not wanting to spoil what was clearly a tender moment. I'd become better at spotting those since learning I was a father. Where before I would have swept into a room without a second thought, only caring about what I needed to say and who I had to say it to, I now took my time. I was courteous, and considerate of people's feelings, in a way I'd never bothered with being before.

I was a neonatal surgeon – or, as my dad called me after my graduation, *Billy big bollocks* – we didn't ask anyone's permission for anything. We simply acted.

It was true what they said, then. Becoming a dad turned you into a poxy softy.

I knew that much was true, because I now had a photograph of Maxina in my locker, an image to spur me on when things got tough. I wasn't just living for the babies in my care, now – I was living for her too. Being a good example to her mattered more than scoring points or thinking i'm the dog's bollocks of neonatal surgeons.

To think I'd ever thought that way now made me cringe.

In the family room, Nina was handing Tabby, our premature baby born in her mother's high school bathroom, to a woman I hadn't seen on the ward before. Lexie was smiling – which was a huge improvement in itself – and was no longer using a wheelchair. Behind the seated woman stood a young boy of no more than 15, watching the tiny baby being transferred to the woman's waiting arms. Tabby was still patched up with tubes and plasters, but she was healthy and thriving, and would soon be discharged.

"There we are. How does that feel?" asked Nina.

The woman looked as though she were holding back tears as she gazed down at the tiny pink infant in her arms. I noticed there were bags of gifts around the place; hats and baby-grows and blankets, as well as more than a dozen cards.

"Like I could burst with happiness," said the woman, letting a tear drop before hurriedly wiping it away. "I'm the world's proudest grandmother."

I realised, then, that the awkward boy standing there was the father of Lexie's baby, and the woman had to be his mother. Relief washed over me, knowing that although Lexie hadn't been able to rely on her own family, she could clearly rely on his.

"Thank you for letting me see her, Lexie," said the grandmother – a very young-looking one, at that – "I can promise you now that you will not be facing this alone. I'll be right here with you, if you want me."

Lexie bowed her head, looking emotional – but she seemed happy, content. It was a shame to interrupt such a moment.

"Nurse Dorrington, could I borrow you for just a second?" I asked.

"Of course," said Nina. "I'll be right back, Lexie."

Nina met me in the hallway, looking bright and pleased with herself. She should be – she'd made that whole scenario possible.

"Nice one, Nina. Looks like it's not all doom and gloom for Tabby and Lexie after all," I said.

"Once Lexie was placed in the mother and baby unit, she gave permission for the boy's family to be contacted. They were shocked at first, but...well, as you can see, Tabby's grandmother is over the moon. I think they're going to be okay," said Nina.

"Looks like it," I said, noticing how Nina blushed and looked away. "Listen, I'm going to need you to scrub-in in about ten minutes. We've a newborn on the way with a build up of fluid on the brain. It looks aggressive, but I'm hopeful. Dr Bellamy will be assisting me – he's hoping to specialise in neurology and possibly neurosurgery, if he thinks he has the stomach for it."

"Of course," said Nina. "I'll see you in there."

♥

Once we were able to look inside the baby boy's skull, I realised this was going to be so much more complex than we'd realised from the initial scans. Not only did a shunt reveal the enormous extent of the fluid build-up, but closer inspection showed the baby had several arteriovenous malformations, or AVMs. They could haemorrhage at any moment, and operating would pose enormous risk of rupture in our attempts to fix them.

Then again, if we did nothing, the baby would most certainly die when one ruptured spontaneously. We could either take the risk now and have some control over it, or wait for the inevitable to happen, and potentially be too late. A brain bleed on an infant this small and delicate would be an impossible situation to manage. AVMs of this multitude were rare in premature babies, and I had to admit this was a unique situation for me.

"The fluid must have obscured these on the scans. I need suction," I said, hoping to bide myself more time to think. Nina produced the suction tube and drew away some of the excess fluid. She replaced the bag for the shunt and took the full bag to be weighed. "Bellamy, let's get another look at the scans," I said.

Dr Bellamy lined them up against the light-board and, indeed, we could see shadows where the other AVMs were hiding. Clusters of veins had gathered in the baby's brain to the point that the scans were barely readable. It was only when we got inside that we could see just how bad it was.

I let out a long, exhausted sigh. This would be an incredibly difficult task and the likelihood was that the baby could not be saved. The question was whether it was worth trying, or whether we should manage the problem with medications and shunts, and only act when a bleed occurred. It seemed unethical, in my experience, to leave it up to chance like that – knowing, as I did, that the baby would be in pain and distress when the inevitable happened.

There was no doubt in my mind that it would occur, and soon.

"Tell me what you're thinking, Tom. Seeing the baby's brain and looking at these scans, what conclusion do you come to?" I asked.

Dr Bellamy sucked in a deep breath. "It seems to me that we're damned if we do, and damned if we don't. It wouldn't be right to leave the baby to take his chances, but interfering would almost certainly result in..."

"Exactly," I said. "And somebody has to explain that to the parents."

Bellamy gulped, knowing that person would be

him – he was, after all, looking to move into this arena once he was ready to. I was contemplating removing that burden from his shoulders, but I knew I shouldn't. Dr Bellamy had explained difficult scenarios to parents before now, but never anything this risky – or dare I say, hopeless. It seemed unfair to put a young budding surgeon in that position.

Then again, I couldn't rescue my own juniors. They'd never learn – and we all had to learn. I damn well had, when I was in his shoes.

"Think you're up to the task?" I asked, perfectly willing to accept whichever answer Tom gave. Only he could say if he was truly ready for this.

Bellamy pinched the bridge of his nose, his eyes taking one last look over the scans and back at the little life on our operating table.

"I'll tell them," he said.

Pride swelled up inside me. Tom was a good lad. I wasn't sure yet if he'd make the best surgeon or not, but when it came to neurology and patient liaison, he was on top form.

♥

I stood by Tom's side as he removed his surgical cap and explained the situation to the baby's mum and dad, who were clutching one another in the waiting room. His mother was in a bad enough state as it was, having just given birth pre-term. She was exhausted, sore, bleeding – and to top it off, her baby was gravely sick. The father looked like a crumpled heap of a man who hadn't slept in a week – and likely hadn't – but he was holding his wife, desperate to keep them together.

"The risks are incredibly high for this magnitude of surgical intervention on an infant so small. However, there *is* a small chance it may work, while leaving it down to fate ensures almost certainly that a bleed will occur and he'll die," said Dr Bellamy. "The final decision about whether to proceed with surgery or wait and see what happens falls with you."

"What kind of choice is that?" said the baby's mother, weeping into the sleeve of her jumper.

The baby's father looked incredulously between Tom and me. "So you're saying our only chance of saving our baby is surgery, right?"

"Yes," said Dr Bellamy. "But the risks are high."

The baby's dad paused, squeezing his wife. "I think we have no choice but to do it. Right, honey?"

The mother nodded as she cried. The baby's father looked between us again, studying our faces.

"Then do what you need to do," he said.

♥

"We're losing him," said Dr Ravi, "His levels are going all over the place. I can't get a grip on him."

"Stay with me, baby," I said. "We've almost got you."

"Water. Suction. Final clip is secure," said

Dr Bellamy, focusing through the binocular microscope. "We should be home and dry now – what the hell is happening?"

"There must be a bleed somewhere," I muttered. "Somewhere we can't fucking see."

"He's bleeding out," said Dr Ravi. "I'm telling you, he's going. I can't stop it."

The room fell silent as the baby's sats dwindled. Then the inevitable did happen. We'd come so very, very close to saving him. A heavy, solemn silence fell over all who were present in the room.

I drew my eyes from the microscope and saw Nina across the way, her dark eyes pooling with tears. I shook my head in despair, telling her it was over. We couldn't save him.

And now, poor Tom would have to tell the baby's parents that the operation had not been a success. I would be right beside him. I'd be his strength if he needed it.

But it wasn't going to make it any easier for us to bear.

# CHAPTER SEVENTEEN
♥

*Nina*

I found him in the break room.

Since that awful day, he hadn't been himself; not his old self, and certainly not his new self. Max had been cold, withdrawn, disappearing after his rounds and making no effort to talk to any of his staff.

Including me.

"Max. I've finally got you on your own," I said, gently closing the break room door behind me. "You've been like a ghost walking through here, like you're on a different plane from the rest of us. What's going on with you?"

He was hunched over in a seated position on the arm rest of the sofa, staring out the window. The view was spectacular, stretching far and wide across London. It was a bright day outside, perfect for another walk in the park.

"Listen, I know the baby's death hit you hard,

but you've got to take it on chin – isn't that what you always say?" I asked. Silence returned to me. Max just kept on staring out that window, lost in thought.

"I thought we could take Maxina to the park today, if you get a break. I noticed your surgical schedule was clear this afternoon. We could go down in your car and pick her up. What do you say?"

Max cleared his throat, bowed his head, and said nothing.

All right – it was one thing ignoring me, but ignoring any suggestions regarding our daughter was bang out of line. I decided I was going to confront him whether he liked it or not. I grabbed him by the shoulder, and he flinched like a scared animal. I stepped back, my mouth dropping open.

"What's with you?" I asked.

"Nina," he said, as if just realising I was there. "Look, I need to be alone for a minute. I need some time to think."

Max stood and pocketed his hands, making his way to the window. He was frowning, deep in thought. Far below, hundreds of people snaked around the city in cars and buses, never knowing that high up in this tower, lives were loved and lost. My heart was with Max, it truly was – and I felt the loss of the baby almost as much as he did. But we both knew that loss of life came with the territory, and this was definitely not our first dance with death.

I had prepared the baby's memory box for his parents, preserving him in photographs, hand and foot prints, and a tiny lock of hair. His box would be stored safely on the ward until his parents were ready to collect it. For some parents, that day never came, and they were never ready to collect their box of memories; but they would be here if they ever did, and that gave those parents comfort. We had boxes that were months and years old, many of them prepared by me.

I had arranged for his little body to be taken to the chapel on-site, where his parents could be with him in peace.

It was the worst, but most important, part of my job. The only way I coped with it was to imagine how bereft the parents were feeling, and to recognise just how much they needed me to keep up my professionalism.

Max needed to remember that – if only I could get it through to him.

"You've been doing a lot of that lately," I said. "Too much of it. You're ruminating, Max. Dwelling. This goes beyond just thinking."

"It's what I need to do to get past it," he said. "Just leave me be."

"Leave you be? With you barely talking to me?" I stepped around Max and leaned in, making it impossible for him not to see me. Still, he kept his eyes on the vista, acting as though he couldn't see me standing right there in front of him.

"What about our agreement, Max? What about our daughter?"

He blinked, and bowed his head.

"This has nothing to do with her," he said, his voice low and melancholic. "I just can't see her right now."

"Because you lost a baby?" I asked. "That's ridiculous. That doesn't make any sense."

"The baby fought hard all the way through. I let Bellamy lead under my guidance, but there was more going on than we could see. I should have referred the baby and got a second opinion before I let Tom in there. I should have led that surgery," said Max, shaking his head. "We rushed into it. We should have taken more time."

"You didn't have time, Max. You said it yourself. This is the loss talking – this isn't logical," I said, holding him by the shoulder. I wanted to knock some sense into him, but I didn't know how.

"Tom's beside himself," said Max, in almost a whisper. "He's been relegated to toxicology and doing the rounds. He's in no fit state for more surgery."

"You can't blame yourself for this," I said. "Tom's a good doctor. He knew the risks."

Max turned and looked at me. "But we didn't know the risks. When we got inside the baby's head and saw the extent of it, I should have taken over. Instead I left poor Tom to experience a catastrophe."

"That's bullshit, and you know it," I said, feeling annoyed with him now for missing the damn obvious. "The surgery was *almost* successful. It had gone well right until the end, and it was nobody's fault. Tom did a great job under your supervision. What happened could never have been prevented!"

"But I won't ever know, will I? I can't explain it to you – your'e a nurse. It eats us up inside. Dr Bellamy will become another bitter, angry loon like me," said Max.

"You're not responsible for Dr Bellamy. He can take care of himself. You *are* responsible for Maxina, though – and for keeping our agreement. You can't just go mute on me when a surgery doesn't go your way," I said, raising my voice. "Look, you're stressed. You're hurting. We've all been there. But it isn't like you to let it affect you like this, Max."

Then I realised *why* it was affecting him so badly. Maxina. He was viewing his work from the perspective of a father as well as a surgeon now, and for the first time in Max's career, it had all become too much.

"I can't deal with it all at once," he said. "I know it's not like me. I know it's not normal. But I simply can't, Nina. If you would just *leave me be and let me think –* "

"You're flaking out on me, aren't you?

You're scared. What about the house you promised our daughter, Max? You're withdrawing communication from me, you're turning down an offer to see your baby in the park. What's next? You're going to go back on the home you wanted to make for her too?"

"Of course I'm bloody not," said Max, almost bellowing. I was touching a nerve, but it was better than speaking to a brick wall. "How could you say that?"

"I'm saying it as I see it," I said. "Because the Max Hartcliffe I know was never this much of a coward. He made mistakes, he saw death, and he carried on. He never let his team down like this."

I needed to get him angry. I needed him to let it all out, or who knows – this kind of reaction was so alien to his usual behaviour that it seemed too risky to do as he asked and just leave him be. Who knew if we'd ever get him back again?

"Fucking hell, Nina. If you want to support me, you'll let me get over this in my own good time," said Max. "Just get out of here, will you?"

"No. I'm not going anywhere. I want you to explain to me why *our* daughter is being pushed aside for your grief."

Max turned to face me, anger flaring up in his eyes like two bonfires.

"What do you want me to say, Nina? That having a kid has changed me? Yeah, it's fuckin' changed me. I'm scared now. Do you understand that? I'm scared. I'm scared of getting this wrong. I'm scared of everything I could lose. I'm scared of seeing that child come through the doors to this very fucking building!"

I was finally getting to him. This was doing him good, I knew it.

"Don't you think that scares me too? Don't you think I've had all those thoughts since before she was even born?"

"Well, what a luxury that must be," said Max. "Some of us were kept in the dark about that."

"We've been over this. You said you never wanted children and didn't even like them – I took that seriously. I was scared, Max. But since we made our agreement, I've kept our communication channels wide open, and all you're doing is shutting them down."

"Bullshit. Leave me alone."

"No, I won't," I said. "I'm not going anywhere."

He gritted his teeth. "I said get out of here, Nina. Go wash out some tubes or something."

"That's it, belittle me. Hurt me. Anything except be a real man about it," I said, realising the moment the words left my mouth that I had gone too far. I was emasculating him.

"Be a man?" he asked, his voice faltering. "Be a fucking man?"

I took a few steps back, rounding the sofa. I'd never seen him this way. His eyes were like a wild animal. He followed me, balling his fists by his side.

"What do you want from me, Nina? You want me to act like some heartless prick to satisfy your idea of what a man is?"

"No," I said, suddenly feeling small. "I want to be sure you'll be there for our daughter. That you'll be a partner to me, like you promised."

Suddenly Max lunged at me, and I wasn't fast enough to avoid him. He grabbed me by the shoulders, his eyes aflame and unrecognisable. As he held me in his grip, he drew my face close to his, so close I could feel his ragged breath on my face. My heart thudded furiously as I awaited what awful things he might say or, worse, what he might do.

The anger in his eyes turned to pain within seconds before me, like shifting desert sands.

"Why won't you just let me be, Nina?" he asked, his voice breaking. "Why can't you let me be? I was *happy* before you stirred all this up in me. Before you brought a child into my world and changed me. Before you fucked me up. *I was happy with my lot!*"

Tears fell from my eyes, and I felt myself shaking.

"No you weren't, Max," I whispered.

He was silent for a moment, taking the words in, still holding me in his vice-like grip. Then he held me around the back of my head and kissed me, hard.

He grunted like a beast and tore at my tunic, and I realised at that moment that there was a hardness pressing against me. Fear leapt through me as he kissed my neck almost violently, as if he couldn't kiss all of me fast enough.

I felt like a rag-doll in the grasp of an enormous beast, completely powerless. I moistened instantly, my nipples hardening to points that could cut glass. Then I found myself pawing at him, my breaths coming quick and fast, as I tore off his shirt and worked frantically at the buckle on his trousers.

Max yanked down my bra, exposing my bare breasts and nipples that longed for his mouth. He groaned as he dove in, squeezing and massaging my breasts as his tongue and lips clamped around my left nub, drawing on me hard.

I moaned involuntarily, muttering that I wanted him, begging him to be inside me. Max lifted his head from my breast and tongued my waiting mouth long, slow, and deep. He held me in his embrace, his hand at my jaw, like he was ready to take all of his aggression and sadness out on me physically, sexually.

And I wanted him to. I was begging him to.

"Nina," he moaned. "I need you."

"I need *you*, Max."

"What the hell is this?" The voice made us spring apart, scrabbling to cover ourselves with our popped-open clothes. In Max's furious ravishing of me, neither of us had even heard the door to the break room opening.

Hannah Shepherd was standing there with a face of pure disbelief.

Max and I glanced at one another as we pulled our clothes back on, unsure of where else to look. I felt the skin on my face flushing beetroot red.

"Oh, now's a fine time to be ashamed," said Hannah, stepping forward into the room. "Wait a minute, it's you. You were a real bitch to me the other day! Deanna told me you were respected all over this hospital – I guess she wasn't wrong. What other rooms have you been respected in?"

"Hannah, get out of here," said Max. "This isn't your business."

She laughed. "No? You're screwing your own nurses and you think it's not my business? We were supposed to be partners. Were you doing this while I was away – is that it? You want to keep up your dirty work rather than join me in the states?"

"I can't be with somebody I don't love, Hannah. I never betrayed you," said Max, straightening his tie.

"What does love have to do with what I just witnessed?" she asked. Then her eyes went wide, looking me up and down again, as if really recognising me for the first time. "Oh god, you're kidding me. This is *her*? This is the woman you had a *child* with?"

So Max really had been telling the truth, I realised. He had told her about Maxina, and told her that he was staying because of her. My heart fluttered and my mind filled with all kinds of thoughts, then. I looked at him and wished we were alone again so I could really show him how I felt. To show him what he meant to me.

"Yes, this is the mother of my child," said Max, sliding his arm around my waist and pulling me close to him. "I'm proud of her. I'm proud of us, and what we've created together."

Hannah snorted. "You're going to destroy your reputation now, you know that? You think I'm going to walk out of here and keep my mouth shut about what I just saw? About your secret love child with your damn nurse?"

"Do yourself a favour, Hannah," Max began, frowning at her as if he didn't recognise the banshee he saw before him. "Get yourself back on that plane and go home, before you get even uglier. All the surgery in the world won't wipe away the picture you just showed me."

I could see by the way her eyes glazed over that his words had stung her. I felt almost bad, knowing that she had to have real feelings for Max, even if she pretended not to. Why else would she be so enraged? I'd never set out to hurt anyone, and I knew Max hadn't either.

"Oh, I'll be going. And I'll be taking your pathetic reputation with me."

Hannah turned and slammed the door closed, leaving us in the quiet room, shaking. Max took my hand in his.

"Look's like the cat's going to be out of the bag, Nina. Are you ready for this?" he asked.

I turned to look at him. "Whatever happens, I'll handle it. Are *you* ready?"

He paused, letting a silence stretch between us. He had more to lose than I did when it came to our career, and word travelled fast amongst the surgeons, with gossip circling hospitals all over the country. I had no doubt in my mind that Hannah would have her revenge.

"I meant what I said to her," said Max. "I'm proud of my daughter. I'm proud of you. Whatever they throw at us, I'll be ready to deflect it. In the meantime, Nina, we've got important work to do."

And just like that, Max ran a hand through his hair, brushed down his jacket, and left the room. Left me, standing there, flustered and confused. Once again I was limbo, unsure of what it was I was really looking for, but knowing damn sure that I was missing it.

But he was right. Of course, he was right.

We did have work to do.

# CHAPTER EIGHTEEN

♥

*Max*

Looks. Stares. Whispers.

Well, Hannah was certainly a woman of her word. She'd told all and sundry about my love-child with nurse Dorrington, and then she'd scarpered on the next plane back to Los Angeles. Should I be relieved to know that I would have at least married an honest woman, even if she did seem like the devil incarnate to me now?

*Never mind*, I told myself. *Keep your head down, get your job done*. It was no bugger's business what Nina and I did, or that we had started a family together. The circumstances of it were immaterial. The fact was that we were making it work now, and that's all that mattered for Maxina's sake.

In fact, I had Nina to thank for that. She'd gotten through to me when I was succumbing to my despair about losing the baby; a reaction I'd never had before, when I was a single man without a family of his own to worry about.

Now that I had Maxina, all of that had changed. Babies weren't just small machines that I needed to fix. They were souls – loved and cherished – and I now knew the fear that all those parents must be feeling when their baby went in for surgery. When I took their children, I carried their world in my hands; their hopes and dreams, the culmination of all their love and devotion. I would never be the same again now that I was a father.

And I realised, now, that was a good thing.

"So let them talk," I muttered, letting myself onto the ward with a wave of my lanyard. The first member of my team that I bumped straight into was charge nurse Deanna, who raised her eyebrows so high they disappeared under her fringe of hair.

"Well, if it isn't Mr Busy," she said, a wry smile lifting the corner of her mouth. "Now, I knew those sparkly eyes on that little girl looked familiar…"

"Shut up," I grumbled, heading for the locker room. "I'm in no mood for you."

Deanna's chuckling followed me as I made my way down the hall. Dr Hurst was in the locker room, tying up her hair. She flushed a furious red and looked away from me, pretending to be looking for a hair tie on the floor.

"It's on your hand, Jennifer," I said.

"Oh? Oh! Would you look at that," she said, her

voice taking on a comical pitch. "I'd lose my head if it wasn't screwed on –"

"Spare me the fakery, Jen. You've heard about my daughter – whoopdy-fucking-do. I've got a repair of a weakened fetal heart valve this morning. Do you want to scrub in and participate in that?"

Her eyes went wide with excitement. "An in-utero operation? Yes, sir, absolutely," she said.

"Good, then stop acting like a moron and act like a doctor," I said.

"Yes, boss. Of course. Thank you for the opportunity," she said, hurrying out into the hall.

I got changed and readied myself for the embarrassment I would likely be feeling on the ward, knowing that it had nothing to do with Maxina or Nina, and everything to do with me. My arrogance could take the hit – it was about time something humbled me, anyway. There'd be whispers and stares, but I could take them. I was a doctor, for Christ's sake. We were above such nonsense.

I only hoped it would be today's news and tomorrow's chip paper, or else my temper might get the better of me at some point or another.

As I left the locker room, Deanna was waiting for me. This time she looked pissed, and I knew she'd already moved on from the scandal. Something operational had got her hackles up.

"Max. This damn refrigerator. We've lost another load of insulin and the maintenance guy is all out of ideas. I need you to approve the budget for the delivery of a new – "

A high pitched whistling sound muted Deanna's voice entirely. I watched her mouth moving and heard no sound of her voice at all. I only saw her face, almost in slow-motion, wincing as if in pain. Locks of her hair swayed around her head.

Down the hall to our left, glass rained down and shattered all over the lino. The force of some explosion knocked us over, leaving us both in a heap on the ground. Deanna grabbed her arm, wailing – she'd hit it at an awkward angle, almost certainly breaking it. I heaved myself up to my feet, staggering slightly. Black smoke billowed from the medicine room. The whistling sound faded as I ran to the source of the explosion.

Nina came rushing toward me, her face bleeding. She'd been struck by broken glass.

"Max, it's on fire! The medicine room – "

I examined her face and was reassured that she was okay, if perhaps in shock. I held her by the arm as we ran to where the blaze had broken out. The large medical-grade refrigerator was now a blackened carcass, while orange flames licked the ceiling.

"Nina, ring the alarm," I said, pulling the fire extinguisher off the wall. Nina set the alarm off, sending a continuous noise off all around the department.

I pulled the key, aimed the nozzle, and sprayed

the Co2 directly at the blaze, sweeping side to side. It dimmed the fire a little, only for it to roar up once again. It was spreading fast, no doubt with the heat source still pumping out fuel for it. The cabinet was wired up to the mains. An immense heat came toward us in a wave, making Nina and I gasp and stagger backward.

"We need to evacuate, Max," she said, her voice shaking.

"Too right," I said, staggering backwards as the blaze rose up to the ceiling and began licking its way out of the open door. Soon the smoke would fill the lungs of every staff member, parent, and baby on this ward.

"Call the fire brigade, tell them exactly where we are. Tell them it's an electrical fire in the east," I told Nina, who nodded and fled down the hall for the nurse's station.

"Right, every body concentrate on my voice!" I bellowed. "We are EVACUATING this ward! Move our vulnerable patients to the CARDIOLOGY WARD. We are in the EAST WING and we are moving them to the WEST WING!"

I cupped my hands around my mouth so my voice carried as far as possible. I paused to help Deanna off the ground, checking she was stable and well enough to follow my instruction. She was hurt, but she was able.

The fire doors would ensure that the fire was contained to this ward as its own compartment.

All of the staff knew the drill and were well trained in moving the babies – even the most vulnerable ones whose machines were helping them to breathe and keep their organs going, though we mercifully had very few of those. They would be kept going via a portable generator until they could be plugged-in when they reached the cardiology department.

"Deanna, repeat what I just said to anyone who can hear and make sure we get everyone out of here. Can you do that? Is your arm too badly hurt?"

Deanna gave me a filthy look as if I'd insulted her. "For a sprain? Get real. YOU HEARD THE MAN, EVERYBODY! MOVE IT! WE HAVE A FIRE ON THE WARD AND WE ARE BEGINNING THE EVACUATION PROCESS!"

I joined Deanna in nursery room one to unhook the two most dependent babies and transport them out of the ward. Nina and the other staff nurses took babies in the additional nurseries and began moving them from the ward, taking them well out of harms way. Dr Hurst and Dr Bellamy took a cot each from ICU, allowing Deanna and I to focus on ensuring everybody was moving out of the ward as instructed.

Confused parents and admin staff, cleaning, catering, and visiting staff members joined the effort to ensure everybody was out and into the west wing, flooding out into the main hall. They were calm, assured, and they followed protocol.

Far from being frantic, I was filled with pride. Our systems were working. Our patients were safe, because we followed our procedures.

The moment we evacuated the farthest end of the ward, closest to the source of the fire, I pulled closed the fire doors and shut it off. That would buy 30 minutes until the fire brigade got here, ensuring the flames and noxious black smoke couldn't spread.

When I was certain everybody had moved over to the west wing, I began doing a head count. All patients were accounted for. All visiting parents that I happened to have spotted as I walked in were accounted for. All the staff members I knew were accounted for.

Except one.

"Where's Nina?" I asked, spinning on the spot, scouring the crowd for her. "Deanna, where's Nina?"

She was cradling her arm, but she was still fighting against it, organising the staff as they moved patients to sensible places in the cardiology department.

"What? Max, what is it?"

"Where's Nina?"

"Nina? I haven't seen her," she said, looking around us.

Then came the sound of a deeper explosion from the east wing, making everybody duck and cower. The sound sent my blood cold as I held my hands over my ears. Whatever overloaded electrical fault had caused the fire in the first place was not finished, and had now blown out the entire room.

"Max, don't you dare go back there –"

Deanna called after me, but I was already running.

I knew it. I knew it in my heart – she was still in there. Nina had for some reason gone back in through the fire doors, and she could already be dead.

The alarm blared above and all around me as I fled through the empty ward in search of Nina, shouting frantically for her. Something told me she was in here; I could feel her. Now I really was in a frenzy, my heart beating out of my chest.

"NINA!" I screamed. No answer.

There was nothing else for it – I had to go in through the fire doors, and I had no idea what level or hell would be waiting for me. No doubt the hall would be filled with toxic smoke that would finish me within minutes, and could have already killed Nina.

Logic told me I shouldn't go in there. I would only be killing myself.

But – *fuck logic*, I thought. I was going in after her. She was the mother of my child. I had to. As I pulled the curtain from around a bay and turned the taps on full blast, images ran through my head of Maxina when she was older, hearing the story of how her mother had died in a fire, and her father hadn't tried to save her. How could I ever look her in those familiar eyes again?

But there was more to it. I realised, as I threw the sodden curtain over my shoulders and covered my back, that I couldn't leave without Nina regardless. It would be agony to lose her, especially without fighting. To abandon her now would ensure that I would not just be grieving, but tortured, if her body was discovered later on. There would be no way I could live with myself if I didn't do everything in my power to save her now.

She was the love of my life.

"NINA!" I cried, pulling open the door. I tucked the wet curtain over my head and dashed inside, crawling as low to the ground as I possibly could.

The hall was dark, the ceiling completely blackened. I shuffled on my hands and knees, coughing. Within minutes I would be dead, but I would die fighting. I knew that now. I would rather die fighting to save the mother of my child than live without her.

But that would mean leaving Maxina. She would have nobody.

"Fuck! NINA! Where are you?" I coughed, an ugly hacking sound, into the wet curtain. If I'd only had time to get some equipment to breath with – but there was no time. And besides, adding a tank of oxygen to a blaze would be a fine fucking idea, wouldn't it?

And that's when I realised, with a sudden wave of horror, what had caused the second explosion. We kept our reserves of oxygen in small tanks in the medicine room. The whole damn room would have blown.

"NINA!" I screamed, beginning to feel delirious. The heat was sweltering, overwhelming; the smoke suffocating. I hit a wall of it and couldn't continue. Failure overwhelmed me; a sinking sadness as I cowered beneath the wet fabric, shielding myself while I could.

*Be a man*, she'd said. *I'm trying, Nina. I'm trying to rescue you.*

Then I felt her. As I shuffled aside, my hand hit a limp foot. I reached and found her leg, her knee, her hand, as fragile as a little dead bird. Immediately I pulled her by the ankles and moved backwards towards the fire doors, dragging her as far as I could. I groaned, feeling weakened by the smoke, using all of my remaining adrenaline to get us out of there.

I threw my back against the door and opened it, hauling Nina through with me. I threw off the sodden sheet and looked at her pale form, checking for signs of breathing. She was breathing – just. Her breaths were heaving, rasping. There was a deep wound on her forehead, and more blood at the back inside her hair. The second explosion must have sent her flying, knocking her out completely.

The sounds of the roaring flames came from behind me, and I was beginning to see things as my delirium increased. Images of Maxina flooded my mind; birthdays, Christmases, graduations. Things I would miss. I saw Nina and me, happy together. I saw us on the beach, holding Maxina, and another little baby – one we might decide to make together, if she and I ever worked out. It was just like the photo of my parents that I used as the wallpaper on my phone; the one that I cherished.

The one that made me believe in love.

Nina had stopped breathing. I had to begin compressions or she would die. But if we stayed where we were, the smoke inhalation we'd already experienced would kill us both.

I picked her up and cradled her in my arms, using the last of my energy to hold her. If the worst happened, I would keep my promise to her, and to Maxina.

"I said I'd be there for you, Nina," I said, my voice a hoarse croak. "I meant it. The house I planned on buying – it was always for you. You and me and our little girl, together. I didn't know how to tell you. I didn't know how to ask you for your love. I just – I just felt it, like arms holding me. If we never make it out of this, Nina, you have to know that I had a place where we would all belong together – you, me, and Maxina. You would never be alone again –"

Smoke was billowing out of the fire doors now, thick and black and noxious. My head was spinning, my eyesight faltering. I tried to lift us both and I couldn't. The heaviness, the weight of it, was all-consuming. My eyes could barely stay open. I looked down at Nina's pale face, her eyes closed, knowing she could have taken her last breaths, and I could be taking mine.

"I love you, Nina," I said, my voice faltering. "You gave me everything."

Some people were rushing towards us from the other end of the ward. Images were swirling in my mind again as they ran to us. I couldn't focus enough to really see them, but I saw yellow helmets, and outfits like hazmat suits. Masks. They were running so slowly, as if wading through treacle.

I saw Nina in my mind's eye, rushing back toward the fire doors once she'd ensured the last of the children and parents were out. I saw her dive inside, knowing where she was going, and what her purpose was. I saw her go flying into the room just inside the hall, where I'd found her. Her hands were reaching up on some shelves for the boxes that had been laying around her body, the ones I felt with my fingertips when I reached for her.

Footprints. Hand-prints. Tiny locks of hair.

Photographs.

These were the memories she'd promised to keep for them until they were ready to collect them. It could be days, weeks, years, and they would be there for them to cherish. Nina had promised them. She would take care of their memories, because she was their nurse.

Because that was all they would have left.

She had gone back for them when the blast hit her.

And now I'd come back for her.

I used every shred of energy I had left to shout for the firemen who were running toward us, believing that they could save her. I had to believe it, if it was the last thought I had. I screamed out as hard as my ruined lungs would allow me.

*"SHE'S HERE!"*

# CHAPTER NINETEEN

♥

*Nina*

Nausea roused me. My head, splitting with pain. Blood drumming hard inside my skull. As my eyes opened lazily, I struggled to focus. Images shifted and smeared as if I was seeing them through a screen of oil. Smears and streaks. Awkward lines. A fun-house mirror. They made me want to vomit. I groaned, curling up, holding my belly.

Voices. Strange sounds that were familiar, comforting.

*Mum-mumumumumum.*

*That's right. Say it again – she can hear you.*

*Mum-mumumumumum.*

*Kiss mummy's head for good luck.*

*I'll take her. You get some rest. You look exhausted.*

*Thanks, Lynn. I think I'll stay here a little longer, just until it gets dark.*

Sharp pains stabbed me in the arms, the neck.

I couldn't move without a stabbing, drawing, or pulsing pain from somewhere. The bed was hot, sweaty, the sheets pulling at me. Was I in bed? *Where* was I in bed?

I sat up, panting, frightened. Glancing around the room, I knew instantly that I wasn't at home. It was a strange, dark, hospital room with an empty chair beside me. I saw the navy blue rectangle of a window, and the slate grey crescent of the moon outside. Something was bleeping. I fell back against the pillow, and once again the sharp pains stabbed me in the wrists, my neck, my groin. I smacked my tongue and lips together; they felt sticky, and far too dry.

"Please," I croaked. "W-water."

"Here you go, hun," came a voice. Liquid beauty filled my mouth; cool and refreshing. I relaxed instantly despite the bleeping, despite the pains, despite the nausea. Despite the looming moon.

"W-where's my baby?"

A soft voice spoke back. "She's with your mother. Try not to worry."

The voice came from a figure leaning over me. I thought it was a woman. She was watching the bleeping screen beside my bed, jotting down notes. High dependency? Was I in a high dependency unit?

"We ran some tests on your urine when you were admitted," said the dark figure. "Did you know that you're expecting a baby?"

♥

As I woke, I realised there was a continuous stream of oxygen filtering through my nostrils. I lifted my sore hand, laden with sticky tape and a cannula site, feeling for the mask on my face. I lifted it off and scratched an itch beneath my nose, wiping off little crusty particles of blood with it.

My legs were bound with tight stockings. A blood pressure monitor swelled and released around my thigh. My chest felt heavy, scratchy, irritable, as if packed with sawdust and sand. Once again, the nausea woke me up – only this time, I really was going to be sick. Saliva rapidly built in my mouth. My stomach tied itself up as if it was wringing out a wet cloth.

"M-m-gonna be sick," I said, belching.

A grey cardboard sick bowl appeared before my face. I hurled into it, my stomach muscles clenching of their own accord, sending pains ripping through me.

"Thank you," I said, and collapsed back against my pillow once more.

Huh. The pillow felt softer this time. No dampness. No bobbles in the fabric. Someone had given me fresh linens.

I drifted back to sleep as I observed the goings-on outside the window. The tops of the trees were bending in a gale. A bird was flitting between the oranges and yellows of the surrounding leaves.

♥

When I woke again, the sky was a slate grey with dark, drifting clouds. Rain speckled the window with droplets that snaked their way down the glass. A cool breeze drifted from the slight opening of the window, through and over me, soothing my broken body. A breath of nature.

This time, I was able to move my head. My heart did a back-flip and made my monitor give a shrill *blip* as I saw who was sitting there next to me, with his head resting on the back of his chair. His eyes were closed, his jaw set, a wrinkle at his brow indicating that he was not having sweet dreams. He'd drawn his arms up to his breast and crossed them. As I reached out with my fingertips to stroke the soft dark fur on his forearm, he gave a little snore. I gently pulled away before I woke him, intending to leave him be and have the pleasure of watching him sleep for a while.

His eyes opened, slightly pink in the corners. He yawned and wiped his face with his hand, glancing my way. He sat up abruptly.

"You're awake!"

"H-how long have you been h-here, Max?" I asked, only managing a whisper. Barely an audible croak. Shock-waves of pain throbbed all the way down my trachea, leaving a burning sensation in my lungs. Breathing in was painful. A strange whistling sound followed as I breathed out.

"Don't speak. Nina. You're still recovering. You were hit by a second explosion – well, almost. The blast knocked you out, and the toxic smoke nearly finished you off." He reached for my hand – a small claw curled up in his warm palm – and rubbed it gently, the motions soothing me. "But I found you, Nina. I told you I wouldn't let you down."

I smiled as my heart swelled. A tear fell from one eye, but I was too weak to wipe it away. Max noticed it and dabbed it away with his finger. He was my hero, my rescuer.

"You've some damage to repair, but you're going to be okay," said Max in a hushed, reassuring tone. "Your mother and I have been managing Maxina between us. She visits you every day."

"Y-you and m-my – ?"

I thought – *he couldn't be serious?*

"Rest, now. Rest," he said, planting a firm kiss on my forehead. "I'm keeping watch over you – as much as I possibly can. I won't leave you here alone. I'm advocating for you – well, doing my best. To be honest I think they consider me to be a bloody nuisance in this hospital. Hardly the rock-star you make me out to be.

"I told them you're a neonatal nurse, and that you put yourself in harm's way for your patients' sake – even though you were so, so bloody stupid for doing that, and we nearly lost you. You did, didn't you? I'm not wrong, am I? I found you, Nina, in that room."

My last movements came back to me in a flash; still unfocused and cloudy, as if my memory was now more damaged than my eyesight. I had thought it was okay, that I could chance it. I would only be quick. The boxes could fit in my arms. There would be no need to lose them; I could keep them safe. Keep my word to their parents.

Then that awful ear-splitting sound exploded between my ears, and I remembered nothing else.

"They were recovered when the fire crew made the area safe to investigate. They're a little damaged on the outside from the smoke, but the contents are safe," said Max. "I brought them back home with me."

"H-how long…has it been?" I asked.

"Six weeks," he said. "A little over. Your body needs to recuperate. You almost – " here his face screwed up, his voice faltering. He looked down at his shoes. "But it doesn't matter. You're here now. You're going to be okay."

I swallowed hard, wincing from the pain.

"Was I burned?"

Max smiled softly. His eyes, like cool pools of water, were made so tender when his face crinkled at the corners like that. He was warmth to me; safety.

"Your skin is as soft and beautiful as it always was," he said. A cool feeling soothed my lips, and I realised it was Max – he was dabbing me with gauze dipped in ice-water. I closed my eyes and enjoyed the sensation of the cool, life-giving water trickling down my throat.

"Do you remember anything I said to you when I found you, pet?" he asked.

Solemnly, I shook my head.

"My memory is a little foggy, but I remember the gist of it. Do you...could you stay awake long enough, do you think, if I were to tell you now?"

I nodded gently, unable to communicate just how eager I was to hear it, whatever it was.

"All right," he said, gently stroking my hair away from my forehead. "Then I'll start at the beginning, and go on from there."

♥

My mother had entered the room at some point with a yipping Maxina, who was excited to see that her mummy was awake.

I drew my parched mouth away from Max's soft, very gently kissing lips, drunk on a heady dose of dopamine. He stroked my cheeks with his thumbs, communicating with his eyes: *I love you, I love you, I love you.*

"Did you tell her about the new house?" asked my mother, sounding a little flustered – it was awkward, no doubt, to find me awake and embracing him. She let Maxina down beside me and I managed to stroke her face, her hair, speaking to her in gentle, but painful, whispers.

"Maxina's ever so excited about it. You should see it, Nina," said my mum. "Your bedroom overlooks the most beautiful English rose garden."

"She will see it, soon enough," said Max. "Now that I know she's foolish enough to want to move in with me."

My body wouldn't allow me to express my love for him; just barely in words, and not even in gestures. I could only lay there, hoping that I could communicate it with my eyes. He gazed down at me with such sincerity that I could be in no doubt at all that he was getting the message.

As the fog of sleep began to roll in and consume me, I realised there was just one thing I simply had to tell Max. It certainly couldn't wait. I gestured with a glance for him to lean in, and he did. As I whispered in his ear, his eyes went wide, startled, his hand squeezing mine.

He looked at me in disbelief, and at that precise moment, my stomach lurched.

"Lynne," he said, his voice shaking and an octave or two higher than its usually low grumble. "Could you – could you pass us that sick bowl?"

# EPILOGUE

♥

*Max*

I cleared my throat, readying for the speech. Though I still used my inhaler, the worst of the smoke damage had mostly faded away. I sucked in a deep breath and got started.

"All right, everybody – gather around."

Deanna. Dr Hurst, Dr Bellamy, our nursing and healthcare assistant teams, all drifted over and made an audience around me.

"You're all aware of the devastating events that occurred best part of a year ago. Well, it gave us all the kick up the arse that we needed to make some much needed upgrades. Our equipment was old and, unbeknownst to us, dangerously faulty, with our electrical points overloaded and buckling under the strain.

"Thankfully, all of the patients and most of the staff...well, you all know how it went. We all made it out, anyway. Never before has the meaning of life, and all that we do here on this ward – every single one of us – been made more clear to me. I'm glad you could join me here today – me, and my beautiful, enormous wife – "

There came a ripple of anxious laughter. Nina dug me in the ribs, shaking her head in disbelief. She looked radiant, truthfully, but the pregnancy was taking its toll on her now that she had gone over her due date. She very definitely wanted this baby out now – and I, for one, couldn't wait to be present when our little boy was born. He would complete our unit, giving Maxina the proud title of Big Sister.

"Anyway, that's enough soppy waffling. I present to you the brand new ICU suite on Little Neptune ward, funded entirely by the generous donations of the public, the parents, and our own members of staff, after an impressive campaign effort led by our dedicated charge nurse."

"Hear, hear!" shouted Dr Bellamy.

Dr Hurst shimmied around us, half-crouching as she lined up her phone for a photograph. I felt awkward, like a prized prat standing there with a big pair of scissors and a ribbon across the doorway – when I should be doing my job – but I understood the sentiment. We were marking a huge development for our ward, with all new state-of-the-art technology installed.

Despite my reluctance to take centre stage and present it, I knew its significance. We were a team, a family. Acknowledging that was important for us, and important for our patients.

"I declare our new ICU...open!" I cut the ribbon to applause, hugging Nina close around the waist.

"Where's Deanna?" I asked, knowing she'd be hiding among the small crowd of staff members and visiting parents. "Come out, you soft thing – we've got a bunch of flowers here to embarrass you with –"

"Max," Nina hissed, tugging at my coat.

"What? Oh she does it all for show, we all know that. She loves having a fuss made of her really," I whispered back.

"No, no – *Max!*"

Nina held the enormous dome of her belly and looked down in dismay as my shoes and scrub trousers were splashed with a gush of amniotic fluid. Panic filled me, taking me by surprise. I hadn't experienced a feeling like it since the fire. The blood drained from my head, and I knew I must have gone a chalky white.

"Oh god, are you all right, Nina?"

She winced, pressing her hands above her thighs, close to the nook of her groin.

"I will be," she said, panting. "But we haven't got long."

Deanna appeared, folding out a wheelchair. She helped Nina into it and glanced up at me, cocking an eyebrow. "Will I need one for you, Dr Hartcliffe?"

I gave her an admonishing look, trying to hide

my fear behind bravado. It was obvious that I didn't have a hope in hell of fooling anyone.

As I rushed Nina away down the hall, toward the central delivery suite, she panted and groaned in her chair. We really didn't have long, and I knew the second baby always came quicker than the first.

"Are you ready for this, Max?" she asked between groans.

"Of course I am," I said. "I've seen babies in conditions a lot worse than childbirth in my time. This should be a walk in the park."

Nina threw her head back and howled with laughter, so hard her shoulders shook. At first I'd mistaken it for a cry of pain, but the laughter almost frightened me. I pushed harder, faster, realising she had to be getting delirious, losing her mind with the pain. She couldn't seem to *stop* laughing.

"What's – what's so funny?" I asked, fearful, in truth, of the answer. I was beyond excited to meet our little boy, and I'd taken care of thousands of babies throughout my career, hadn't I? So what was I missing?

"This isn't surgery. You don't take this one back to the recovery room and get on with the next job. If you thought *Maxina* was a surprise - " Nina paused as another contraction claimed her. She clutched the arms of her wheelchair and arched her back against the surge. She breathed out once it was over, sweat building on her brow.

She smiled, remembering what she was going to say.

" – then you really, *really* don't know what you're in for, Max Hartcliffe," she said. "Get ready to have every facet of your personality tested; everything you ever thought you knew about yourself to be ground into a paste by a tiny, needy, screaming –"

Nina arched her back and began to wail, long and low.

"Nina?"

She rolled her eyes, her head lolling as the contraction relaxed again. They were so close together now; the baby would be delivered in minutes.

"Oh Max," she said, in a sardonic, all-knowing tone that sent a shiver of fear up my spine. She reached for my hand and held it tight. "You'll find out soon enough."

## THE END

# ABOUT THE AUTHOR

## Liza Collins

Liza Collins is a wife and mother of two boys from the UK. She writes erotic romances to explore her fascination with assertive, intelligent, dashing heroes and the firecracker women who get their ties in a twist.

Visit www.LizaCollinsBooks.com to find out more.

# SACRED HEART CHILDREN'S HOSPITAL

## Book 2: The Intern And The Plastic Surgeon

"When I made the leap to children's plastic surgery, Dr Wes Brookes fast became my idol. Now he wants me to be his fake fiancé to spare him from his prying family. How can I tell if my wildly-growing feelings for him are real, or part of our performance?"

Senior plastic craniofacial surgeon Wes Brookes is fierce, dominant, and leads the world in children's plastic surgery. His grumpy exterior hides a soft underbelly – after all, he has his own facial disfigurement, so he knows what it's like to grow up feeling different.

When he asks me to be his fake fiancé, what starts as a favour to win points fast becomes a big, big risk for my career. I think I'm falling fast for the man behind the mask, and my own façade is slipping. How can I succeed in my internship if I fall in lust – or maybe love – with the man who is supposed to teach me everything?

Besides, he's so close with his staff nurse; she knows him inside-out and back-to-front. I don't want to come between them and their bond, but our fake relationship is starting to get hot...and very, very real.

Get ready for some big grumpy fake fiancé drama in the plastics department of Sacred Heart Children's Hospital, London. A love triangle, a fake fiancé, and a grumpy-sunshine dynamic against a backdrop of children in need of life-changing surgery.

Wes Brookes knows all about faking it; he crafts new faces every day. But when a false relationship creates some very real chemistry, will he be bold enough to drop the act and let love in?

# BOOKS BY THIS AUTHOR

**The Nurse And The Neurosurgeon: Professionals Gone Wild, Book 1**

Smoulderingly-hot, tall, dark, grumpy, super-wealthy neurosurgeon? That's Silas Griffin. He was flying high until his beloved wife passed away, leaving him a widowed single dad who's married to his career. Who has time for love when there are lives to save, anyway? Silas needs a voluptuous auburn-haired vixen to stir up trouble in his department like he needs a head injury, but when Zoe joins his team of nurses, his instant attraction could make him lose his mind all together.

Fiery, lusty, with her heart on her sleeve - Zoe is a dedicated nurse who lives an eclectic and free-spirited lifestyle, but she's also one big commitment-phobe after her terrible divorce from Euan. It'll take Zoe a long time to trust again. When she joins the neurology ward, she can't help longing to turn up the heat with the tall, dark and moody neurosurgeon. Zoe wants to get inside his heart, his head, and his pants – but will her commitment issues prevent the sparks between them from igniting?

Silas and Zoe rely on their professionalism for survival in a cruel world, but what happens when their passions go wild in the workplace? Can their careers survive being blind-sided by love?

## The Suit And The Signorina: Professionals Gone Wild, Book 2

Tall, ripped, dangerously hot – with a trust fund that makes his Investment Banker salary look like small change – that's Jack Dickens. He's got it all, with a secure future mapped out for him by his banking mogul father. His only problem? He wants to throw it all away. Jack thinks becoming a delivery driver will get him closer to nature and the simple life, while his father works to ensure that he never leaves his gilded cage. When Jack falls for Italian beauty Isabella, the stakes get exponentially higher. Will Jack leave the life he knows behind and go totally broke for love?

Feisty, independent, and Milan-runway-gorgeous, Isabella likes to live fast and free . Since the death of her darling Papa, she's determined to never invest in love again. She's already lost too much and besides, she promised him that she'd explore all life has to offer with no ties. Isabella needs an ungrateful yuppie in her life like she needs a punctured tyre, but her dormant desires are ignited when rebellious Jack shows he's more than just a daddy's boy; he's a hot-blooded man out to prove himself, and Isabella just became his muse.

Jack and Isabella are two lost souls with white-hot chemistry between the bedsheets. Will their differences separate them forever, or will destiny ensure these unlikely lovers find a home in each other's arms?

## The Barrister And The Bridesmaid: Professionals Gone Wild, Book 3

Devilishly handsome, sharp-witted, playboy billionaire barrister – that's Linus Griffin. He's never seen any necessity for love. Why, when he could have a fling and get back to what he does best: prosecuting. Linus doesn't count on one of those flings rocking his world at his brother's wedding, and returning a year later in his witness box. Not only that, but she's his brother's chief bridesmaid and brand-new sister-in-law – surely, she's off-limits? Why, then, does he find it impossible to keep away from the forbidden fruit?

Strong-willed, darkly beautiful, career-driven social worker – that's Clara Murphy. She lives for her clients, but when one such client leads her to the witness stand, she can't believe who's grilling her – none other than the hot barrister she bagged at her sister's wedding. Clara has no time for love, but when she spies her barrister at a wild, invitation-only party, their masks make it all too easy to play-pretend. A sharp dose of reality strikes them both when Linus intercepts Clara's stalker – a man he sent to prison – and finds his place at the bar in jeopardy. They must choose whether to admit defeat and part ways, or face the fire together as one.

Can Linus and Clara ever commit to love when the careers they're so devoted to might just be what tears them apart?

Printed in Great Britain
by Amazon